T0149488

Curious Reflections

Or

Drama Llamas and Llama Dramas

A sort of novel by

Lesley Zobian and Ann Humm

iUniverse, Inc.
New York   Bloomington

Copyright © 2009 by Lesley Zobian and Ann Humm

All rights reserved. No part of this book may be used or reproduced by any means, graphic, electronic, or mechanical, including photocopying, recording, taping or by any information storage retrieval system without the written permission of the publisher except in the case of brief quotations embodied in critical articles and reviews.

iUniverse books may be ordered through booksellers or by contacting:

iUniverse
1663 Liberty Drive
Bloomington, IN 47403
www.iuniverse.com
1-800-Authors (1-800-288-4677)

Because of the dynamic nature of the Internet, any Web addresses or links contained in this book may have changed since publication and may no longer be valid. The views expressed in this work are solely those of the author and do not necessarily reflect the views of the publisher, and the publisher hereby disclaims any responsibility for them.

ISBN: 978-1-4401-9094-0 (sc)
ISBN: 978-1-4401-9095-7 (ebook)

Front cover design by Emma-Lee Taaffe

Printed in the United States of America

iUniverse rev. date: 12/14/2009

To Chris, Nic and Les (Dad)
with love and apologies
(Please don't sue!)

Chapter One

It was as I staunched the flow of blood from the bite I had received from a short but lively skirmish with the ferret as I tried to clean out his bedding and he informed me, in no uncertain terms, that he did not wish his bedding to be disturbed and that I should go away and bother somebody else, that I began to question the dynamics of the animal/human relationship. In particular my own relationship with animalkind.

At one time I had been under the comforting delusion that we are supposed to have dominion over the animals. A few years in the countryside had made me doubt, in fact I was slowly coming to the uncomfortable conclusion that far from us being in charge, animalkind did very well on its own, thank you very much, and that they had in fact developed a way of manipulating us (me) to do their bidding. Instead of sitting back enjoying nature, I find myself looking anxiously out of the window hoping the bird feeders are well stocked in order to avoid the accusing glare of blue tits sitting on my windowsill staring in at me, plotting to use my car for bombing practise and raiding my milk bottles for the cream. Or making sure I have put food right down the bottom of the garden for the badgers so that they will not come up near the house and dig up my flower bed, uprooting the magnolia and laying out my prized dahlias as a warning. And then there's the heron who, without any provocation at all, will regularly come and empty my fish pond.

When I share these feelings with neighbours, they look at me with pity. Some even sneer. They are country people, born and bred, and the local fauna apparently know this and have a healthy respect for them and their property. I, on the other hand, am an "incomer", a soft townie wandering innocently into the countryside, and therefore fair game for threat and manipulation.

It seemed like a good idea at the time. Move away from London and buy a cute little cottage in the country with just enough land to indulge in a spot of bucolic living. Grow vegetables. Have a few hens scratching about the place. A hive of bees. Even buy a couple of alpacas to graze in the paddock.

Seven years on and the dream is wearing a bit thin. Quite frankly I have had enough of battling with flaming alpacas who insist on eating everything that springs greenly from the ground or reddishly on a tree. Mowing grass that insists on growing even more vigorously just as soon as I've put the lawn mower away. Pulling up weeds that fling their seeds out over my shoulder as I cart them off to the compost heap. Hens that do not confine themselves to the vast area of lawn and paddock, but who insist on scratching up seedlings and newly springing vegetables.

And I am particularly fed up with myself for having Good Ideas about how to make the garden look better.

Stuff this so-called Good Life. I want a mud hut with a window box.

I was sitting out in the brief spell of surprisingly intense sunshine we had the other day and my eye roved about over the garden around me. I was sitting on the flagged area that I optimistically call the patio looking across to the large lawn where the dogs are allowed to run and where the hens should confine themselves (but don't). Through a little arch there is also another bit of garden which I call my "secret" garden for no other reason than that it is surrounded by a fence and hedge and therefore cannot be overlooked. It has a pond and is rather pretty, and as it is so sheltered I like to sit there when I get some time to myself. The trouble is, it is a very small area. Two weekends ago I had a little gathering around the barbie in the secret garden to celebrate the first warm day of the year, and quite frankly it was ridiculous – elbows in the face, nowhere to sit, etc. I know, I know, I should have used the big lawn for such an occasion, but, well, I didn't. OK? So I got out my drawing paper and started making plans to create another, very beautiful, bit of garden where dining would be a more leisurely and comfortable affair. It would have a lawn, and a pond, and a little curved path, and a raised flowerbed. I felt quite enthusiastic about the project and eager to get construction under way.

On Friday I bought twelve old railway sleepers for the construction of the raised flowerbed.

Twelve.

Railway sleepers.

Twelve.

I borrowed a truck from work and the man at the builders' merchants kindly fork lifted them on. So far, so good. Back home I now had to unload the railway sleepers by myself. All twelve. And stack them. Then return the truck. Then come home and site the railway sleepers. Twelve railway sleepers. By myself.

Of course it's not just a question of siting the sleepers, there is also the small matter of levelling the ground first, and digging up any turf and weeds that I thought might grow upwards through the soil and sprout in the new bed. And it was hot, very hot, on Friday, even though it was so early in the year. Taking a deep breath and metaphorically girding my loins, I set about my task. It took a great deal of heaving and toiling, along with some considerable grunting and groaning, but I worked steadily and eventually got the darned things into place. It was then a mere matter of hauling out the bags of compost I had set aside to fill my new flowerbed.

Red-faced, decidedly raw and sore on the shoulders from the burning sun, and sweating in a most unladylike manner, I finally sat down in the cool of the conservatory adjacent to the kitchen to admire my handiwork through the window and down a very large glass of water, swiftly followed by a celebratory G&T or two. It was as I was relaxing that Reeb wandered into the kitchen, sniffed the air and remarked happily:

"Ah, roast for dinner tonight."

You know you're in trouble when your daughter thinks there is meat roasting, and you know there is nothing in the oven ......

On Saturday, the G&T's and a good night's sleep having blurred the memory of the previous day's toils, I decided that a pond would complement my new raised flowerbed a treat, so I marked out a rectangle on the ground with sand. I had grand ideas to start with. A nice big pond, I thought, possibly with some kind of water feature, a fountain in the middle, perhaps, or maybe a small waterfall. But as I began to dig and my muscles suddenly remembered the abuse I had given them the previous day, my enthusiasm for such opulence waned rapidly.

After about half an hour of battling with good Bedfordshire clay which had been gently baked by the sun for the past few days, I amended the size of my rectangle to a modest two and a half metres by one and a half, and decided that a depth of forty-five centimetres would be more than enough. As I dug I also discovered that some previous owners of Weasel Cottage had apparently decided to use the back garden as a rubbish dump for old asphalt (from the drive before it was overlaid with stones, I think), quarry tiles (the old kitchen floor), whole and broken bricks (who knows), and, believe it or not, lots of china and old glass bottles. Emma-Lee, or Small as we call her, loved it! She pretended we were on an archaeological dig and tried to piece together bits of old china to make plates and cups.

You're so easily pleased when you're nine, aren't you?

Well I have to admit that about three inches down I gave up. I limped over to the chalet at the bottom of the garden where my son, Kester, lives and explained to him, in very careful language, just why he ought to help his old mother out. I think there may have been mention of "open road", "all your stuff in a suitcase" and "I brought you into the world, I can take you out" woven through the cajolery to suggest his fate if he did not comply with my request. Of course the last threat was empty since at that particular moment in time I did not have the strength to squash a small fly had it landed on a delicate part of my anatomy and proceeded to do a vampire act, let alone do any sort of violence to a six foot something eighteen-year-old. Still, give the Boy his due, he rose to the occasion, fished out a pick axe (the existence of which I had been unaware), stripped off his shirt and got going on the hole.

I must say that getting Kester involved in garden projects is always a Last Resort. He is an apprentice engineer. Part way through his excavations he paused, cast a glance at my beautiful raised flower bed and announced that it was "out of true". He said it sloped and widened. I said, somewhat tightly, that I knew it widened. I wanted it like that, and as for not being level, well I'd done my best. He all but sneered. He fetched out his spirit level, squinted, tutted and sighed and cast me a despairing look. I said, defiantly, that it was Good Enough. It was only out by an inch. But apparently in engineering terms an inch may just as well be a mile. It was Out. I told him (smiling very politely) that the flower bed was absolutely fine. It was rustic. And the point of a rustic flowerbed is that it has to be ad hoc (I liked that phrase). If gardens were too regimented they would look wrong (I have used this argument before. Roughly translated it means "Blow that for a game of soldiers, I've had enough of digging/levelling/measuring/smoothing/etc and want a Martini!" or "What do you mean clean all those garden pots? – they're meant to be covered in moss/grime/bird poo/etc – they're rustic! Hedges also look better rustic.

So do garden chairs, flower beds, shrubs, ponds, bedrooms, bathrooms, kitchens – you see where I'm going here?). And anyway, I continued to Kester, once the plants grew up and hung artistically over the edge you would hardly see the railway sleepers at all.

Kester opened his mouth to say something more, so I got in quickly with a warning that if he had anything else to say on the matter we would all discover just how far up a rectum an ungreased spirit level would go (I was feeling my strength returning by now).

Without a word Kester got back to his digging.

So things progressed. The pond was dug and lined and filled. I put some flowers in the raised bed and I widened the patio area a little, but now realised that all the slabs actually needed to be removed, the ground levelled and the slabs replaced. I could not face that task right then – and I dared not ask the Boy and his Spirit Level for at least a week or so.

In an attempt to keep my mind off other projects, and to give myself a legitimate excuse to ignore all the housework that was shouting out to be done and to sit down for a while, I decided to log on and see if there were any e-mails from Ann. Ann, or Mowl as she is known, is a very diligent correspondent, keeping me up to date with all the trivia and goings on down in her neck of the woods.

She is known as Mowl because when we were children we would amuse ourselves by deciding what animals people reminded us of. Because of her short-sightedness and penchant for black velvet, Ann was of course a mole, hence Mowl. For reasons we shall not go into, I was a ferret, or Pherrit (somehow the "ph" makes it seem so much better). This form of nicknaming persisted into adulthood with the result that Ann's husband Chris is known as Lam (because of his blond, tightly curling hair), and my son Kester is called the Owlmaster. This last name came about, not because Kester looks anything like an owl, but because of my (admittedly reprehensible) penchant of telling scary stories to the children at bedtime when they were very little. I used to regale the diminutive Small with tales of yellow-eyed owls who would come tap, tap, tapping on the window in order to sneak in and eat the toes of little children as they slept. As I was leaving her bedroom one night I noticed her large, frightened eyes watching me as I went, and I took pity on her and said that she need not worry since her big brother was actually the Owlmaster who would protect her from the owls. She was much heartened by this knowledge, and the nickname stuck.

Actually I should be careful how I treat Small. I know that my ultimate fate rests in her hands. Some years ago I had remarked cheerfully that I was glad I had four children as this meant I was sure to be looked after in my old age. Apparently this struck fear into the breasts of my beloved offspring, no doubt due in no small measure to my avowed intent to become an eccentric and difficult old woman (I believe I heard Jay mutter something along the lines of "So no change there, then."), selectively deaf and always bearing a sharpened walking stick with which to attract attention. A few days after my innocent remark I came home to find that the three oldest children had got Small (aged three at the time) into a corner and were rolling her thumbprint over a contract which apparently stated that she promised to take full and final responsibility for me in the event that I become in any way incapacitated, be it through illness, accident or old age. I have to admit that I was impressed with the comprehensive language used in the contract, and my chagrin at being thus shuffled off was somewhat mitigated by the thought that one of my children could well have a flourishing career in the legal profession. An idea as to how I could ensure financial security in my old age leaped into my mind. I immediately began keeping a diary in order to record any events which could be used as blackmail material when they were eventually successful, "in the money" and perhaps ready to branch into politics.

So, with that contract in mind, I know that I ought to be kind to Small. It could well be that she will be the one sitting by my bedside in those final hours, and hers the last voice I hear as she triumphantly, and probably with considerable relief, commands the doctors to "Switch her off".

Anyway, as I had hoped, there was indeed a message on my computer from Ann.

"What ho to the Old Boot!" *It read. I do appreciate the love and respect I receive from my little sister.*

"Just thought I'd drop you a line to let you know how we got on at the riding stables the other day and our little trek across the moors. I was rather hoping that riding would be a leisure activity that Lam and I could share, but I have now had second thoughts. It appears that Lam and horses do not mix. He has ridden twice in his life, and has been bitten on both occasions. It's his blond (i.e. invitingly straw coloured) hair that attracts them, I'm sure. Either that or he is so pale they mistook him for a tasty bit of turnip! Whatever the cause, Lam prefers wheels, pedals, and above all – *brakes* to four hooves, lots of teeth and a mind of its own. Still, all credit to him, he knew that I liked the idea of horse riding, so he was willing to at least give it a go.

We enter the stable area. Quite a bit of neighing and hoof stamping.

I was OK. My sweet little Nutmeg was clearly on Valium and I had a peaceful, if uneventful ride. We had an arrangement, Nutmeg and I: she would amble about for a while and get me home in one piece, and I would not cry. I was hoisted aboard first and joined the other novices plodding slowly around a paddock just so that we could get used to our mounts. The trouble is that most of the horses sussed immediately that they had novices – or suckers – aboard and decided to eat, not plod, and of course we were all too polite (or scared) to yank up their heads and get them moving. (Or perhaps just too British. We just can't seem to be firm with animals for fear of hurting them, can we? 'I say, would you mind just raising your head for me? ...... Er, he doesn't seem to want to go. What should I do?')

Lam, on the other hand (or hoof) was the last to be mounted. I had seen this horse off to the side and, judging by the way it was rolling its eyes, sidling and attempting to kick out, had assumed (wrongly it now appeared) that it was to be ridden by our guide. I watched with a mixture of surprise, worry and (I guiltily admit) glee as Lam was hoisted aboard.

No brakes.

'Whoa! Whoa!'

Skitter, prance, wail!

And off we went.

Lam was taken to the front as he clearly had the alpha male who was not going to trail quietly behind any string of plodders, uh-uh, not this Cookie! And as I was, nominally, with Lam, I came next. Well. Real McCoy (Lam's mount) wanted to GO! Anyone ahead (a small matter of our guide) could be ridden down and trampled! We had already been told to keep a couple of feet (not hooves) from the horse in front (or as our guide cheerfully put it: 'No butt sniffing now!'). Real McCoy was not interested in sniffing any butts. He had his choleric eye set on the wide blue yonder! Every now and again the guide would pause to check behind him, usually to call back (a long way back) to me:

'Lady, get her to go faster. Move her on a bit!'

Following which admonition I would dig little Nutmeg in the ribs (but not too hard, you understand) and, rather than just quicken the walk a little, which would have suited yours truly just fine, she broke into a trot. And when you do not expect it, and have not 'bumped' properly for years, a sudden violent trot is not something you, or your butt, relish very much. Meanwhile, in front of me I saw Real McCoy trying to muscle passed the guide's horse, but it seems that he too may well have been an alpha male, and objected strongly to the hassling with a few well placed kicks as the two horses jostled for possession of the path.

And so we reached the top of the tor where we took a little time out. Here either one of the guides took pity on

Lam, or else they were concerned about their insurance, but either way Real McCoy was taken off, run up and down the hill a few times, apparently to wear him out a little, and generally 'whispered' to. Lam did some whispering, or rather muttering, of his own.

Did Real McCoy calm down? My eye he calmed down! So he was led off and Lam was mounted on Silver Currency. At last – a slug!

Nutmeg had now either a) woken up, b) smelled her hay bale, or c) was due for her next dose of Valium. Whatever it was, she was a little (not excessively though) quicker going back and it was Lam (now following me) who kept on being told:

"Get him to go faster. Move him on a bit."

But Lam was now happy and was not about to rock any boat, horse or any other vessel you cared to name. Slow is good.

After that we retired to a little pub we had spotted during our trek, and a swift half of lager and lime revived the parts other lagers fail to (and do not wish to) reach. It was not necessarily the old bot that hurt after all that riding! – I will say no more.

So, reluctantly, riding is off the agenda. Will have to think of something else.

Ta ra for now

Mowl

PS: So spring has arrived in the grey and gloomy depths of Bedfordshire, has it? I consider it the very nadir of base perfidy that you should rub my snout in the fact that you 'spent too much time gardening' when the nearest we came to gardening was to stare through the rain washed windows and look at some seed catalogues (waterlogues?).

I am going to plant rice.

And a plastic sunflower."

I do enjoy Ann's e-mails. It's always good to hear that someone else's life isn't all plain sailing. Or riding. And it is also a mild comfort that I can sometimes make her jealous.

Chapter Two

It's funny how real some dreams can feel. This one had been prompted by my step-mother, Marie, asking if I could obtain a tin of adzuki beans for her since the shops around her in North Wales didn't stock such exotic fare, and the fact that I have recently been thinking about a distant relative of mine called Great Uncle Horatius and his companion Stinky. The Great Uncle and friend, having private means, some skill at gambling (or at least cheating at cards) and an eye for the main chance, spend their time exploring the lesser known regions of such places as the Congo and Borneo, and generally getting into scrapes. The aged relative then regales me with tales of their exploits by means of postcards sent from obscure destinations, but I have not heard from him or Stinky for quite some time now.

Ann disowns Great Uncle Horatius. In fact Ann maintains (quite vociferously) that he cannot be a blood relative of mine and not a relative of hers, and that this proves that he is but a figment of my imagination and that the missives I pass on to her are utter rot. I have argued indignantly that he is indeed real, but then, I have to concede, what is reality? Some contend that everyone outside of Self is a figment of Self's imagination. Who is Ann? Who is Chris? Why do I waste my time writing drivel to them? Have I even written anything?? Following such arguments I then exhort Ann to accept that Great Uncle Horatius is indeed a reality, and a thorn in the side to boot. And I will not be questioned further on the matter. This allows me to trump her in the "interesting e-mail" stakes when life gets a bit tedious.

Anyway, back to the dream, it seems that my subconscious decided that I was going to track these beans down, no matter what the difficulty. So, with nothing but a rough blanket, a tooth brush and some beads for bartering, I set off on alpaca-back down to Dover where, after a small argument with the quarantine and customs officials, we boarded a ferry to Spain. It was a rough crossing and both the alpaca and I spent most of our time below decks praying for death.

It did not come, however, and upon sober reflection we were both rather grateful for that fact.

Disembarking in Bilbao we ignored the toots and curses of the crowds of trucks and cars as we ambled along the road with our very own tail-back, and struck out southwards. The weather grew warmer and I had to stop off at a little farm to have the alpaca shorn since the smell of rancid alpaca was beginning to make my eyes water. As I was able to sell the fleece in the village this also provided me with a little money with which to buy food as I had been foolish enough to start on this journey with nothing more than one cheese sandwich, two pieces of liquorice shoe-laces, which were tangled in the lining of my coat pocket, an apple, a bottle of Dr Peppers and a pickled onion. The alpaca had much to say about the smell of the pickled onion on human breath, and the effects of fizzy drink on the digestive system, but I will not bore you with it. Apparently my comments about the stink of rancid alpaca was still rankling.

(As an aside at this point, I think I could have made more money by selling the talking alpaca rather than just a common or garden alpaca fleece, but there you go. We live and learn)

Onward, then, to Morocco where we slipped across the border by fording a river that was a little fiercer than I had anticipated, and picking our way through a mountain pass, nervously avoiding rock falls and bandits. We came eventually upon a sleepy, fly and flea-ridden little town where we could rest for a while. I caught up with some much needed sleep in the shade of a rather gnarled acacia tree, and as I did so the alpaca (evidently having more business sense than me) took advantage of my unconsciousness and slipped away down a back alley with a black-coated, shifty-eyed Arab. There some heated negotiations took place as the alpaca tried to sell me for a bale of hay, a large straw hat and a small harem of comely sheep. The Arab, however, looked me over as I slept, spat noisily, and apparently offered a handful of grass and a pair of secondhand (second-foot??) sandals made out of an old rubber tyre. Unimpressed by the fact that the sandals were made from Firestone's finest and were guaranteed not to slip in wet weather, even when cornering, the alpaca haughtily refused the deal.

It is very lowering when one finds out one's real worth.

As we crossed the border into Algeria (there was now quite a bit of tension between us, I have to say) we almost immediately stumbled upon an open air market, gay with colourful awnings sheltering the merchants from the fierce heat of the sun. After I had made reparation for the damage we had done by trampling much stock during said stumble, I had leisure to look around – and, lo! – there, in the corner, tucked away behind a man selling fried locusts and another trying, with a sharpened stick, to persuade a small boy to shin up a rather precariously swaying rope while his mate played on a warbling flute something which sounded suspiciously like "Danny Boy", there (as I've said) was a tiny stall laden with tins of adzuki beans!

With a joyful cry I parted with a gold nose ring and the two pieces of liquorice shoe-laces, tucked two tins of beans into the saddlebag, and turned the alpaca's head for home. Luckily the rest of his body followed, and it was but a short time before we were back in good old Blighty with the bells of London's churches ringing jubilantly, if discordantly, in our ears.

It was a bit of an anticlimax to open my eyes and find

that the ringing was nothing more than my alarm clock and that reality was a grey day in April with nothing more to look forward to than a dreary day at the office.

Felt a bit flat today. Didn't particularly want to come in to the office, but you know how the old bumper sticker puts it: I owe, I owe, so off to work I go.

Not many people in the factory today. Mike the Foreman is away, which means that the other chaps are skulking about down in the lower workshops chatting and drinking tea and probably working on their own projects. Richard is out of the office for the morning (hooray!), so I do not have to listen to another saga about thermocouple dock leads failing due to pseudo atmospheric pressure building up in the algorithmic turbo transducer which connects the flange socket to the main haemorrhoidal torus output feed – and we all know what *that* means. I tell you, no man has ever used so many incomprehensible words on so many boring subjects – and he can keep it up for hours. Even when I'm obviously on the telephone he mooches up to my desk, hands in pockets, huge frame hunched over like a circus armadillo balancing on its hind legs, and starts mumbling at me.

That's another thing: Richard mumbles. I long ago gave up trying to understand what he says by straining forward, brow furrowed listening intently and asking "Pardon?" every now and again. The trouble is you can't ask "pardon" too often because then it makes you seem dumb, so you have to use the pardon word at junctures where you know you've got at least some hope of understanding whatever it is when it's repeated. And that's an art in itself. Anyway, now I just smile sweetly when Richard talks, and think of Other Things.

Sometimes I try to escape by nipping off to the toilet. But that doesn't work. I hear him loitering outside, scuffing about and pretending to pinch the dead leaves off plants until I emerge so that he can continue the (one-sided) conversation.

I don't know why he wants to talk to me. All he gets

is interested grunts and ah-ha noises, and lots of eyebrow movement. Eyebrow movement is a good ploy when you don't actually understand what it is you are listening to and it's not vital that you do. Also, the odd, very slow nod of the head. And if you really want to impress, add a short crack of laughter every now and again as this suggests you are acknowledging, and applauding, a particularly clever comment and is sure to convince the talker that you are just as up-to-date and knowledgeable upon the subject as they are – possibly even cleverer if you inadvertently put the laughter in an inappropriate place. They are bound to think that you have spotted something that has escaped them.

But Richard is not here for a few hours (that deserves another Hooray!). He has gone to the airport to collect a Russian chap who is going to look over one of our machines. I think Richard has been watching too many bad spy movies. He left here in a trench coat with the collar turned up and a trilby slanted down over his eyes, and I saw him practising his goose-stepping as he went off down the path to his car. I must say he looked rather resplendent in a fine false bushy moustache, except that it kept falling off and looking like some kind of hairy tarantula as it clung to his collar or shoulder. I'm rather hoping Richard will be whisked away by the airport police as an illegal alien for a bit of interrogation and probing – especially the probing.

The thought cheered me up considerably.

It's nice to have the office to myself for a while. Nic isn't due in until about midday. It's funny how being alone in a public place puts odd thoughts into your head. I wandered about the offices and began wondering if I could risk shedding my clothes and skipping naked through the rooms whistling the Blue Danube and doing the occasional shimmy. But it is far too cold for that, it is, after all, only April and the brief, glorious heatwave we had recently is now but a glittering memory. So I didn't. And anyway, it could well be the window cleaner's day to call.

Had a couple of interesting e-mails at work. There was

a very esoteric enquiry from a customer of ours in Hungary which went as follows:

"Hello!

I hope for it pleasantly the Easter passed by.

I had a little problem with the turbine sent last year.

On the axis of the generator being wedge sheared and the rotor of the generator got ruined. The ribbed hole cracked in what it is a wedge orbit, yes. The crowned mother and the cotter pin were on him on the axis, and after all could loosen!

I send some pictures to you in order for you to be allowed to study him.

Regards – Zoltan"

Sounds like a West Country escapee with all these references to the turbine as "him". I just hope the chaps in the workshop can work out the problem from the pictures. Personally I like the idea of the crowned mother, although I don't see that as a problem since the cotter pin is apparently on him, not her.

There was another e-mail from a customer in the Netherlands. The previous day he had enquired about an elbow for an air hose pipe. Nic had replied that although we didn't stock that item, he could obtain one from someone who had described it to him as being "removed, but in mint condition". Today, presumably after some consideration and much discussion amongst his colleagues, our baffled Amsterdam customer asked:

"Please, what is mint condition? Is it the colour?"

A delicately tinted mint green elbow pipe, how wonderful!

Such messages lighten my day.

Made my way home through the driving rain wondering who had stolen spring. My new pond is full to overflowing and the plants in my new raised flowerbed are looking decidedly sad and bowed down. I glanced at it as I walked towards the house and of course now all I can see is just how much it slopes and widens.

Darn Kester and his engineer's eye.

Stood looking disconsolately out of the kitchen window as I filled the kettle and listened to the overly-cheerful BBC weather girl informing us that we're in for a lot of blustery and rainy weather this week which is being swept up from the south west. Since she has moved to Cornwall Ann has come to realise just how much in rains down there. She has come to the conclusion that most of the cumulo-nimbi head for south-west England as their preferred destination. Cornwall then squeezes them dry and passes them on to us.

I'm not so sure about the squeezing dry bit.

Ann also made a little comment once about God making sponges and spaniels on the same day, both soak up considerably more than their weight in water. I think my alpacas overheard the comment and saw it as a challenge. As I looked out of my window I could see them standing forlornly in their field as the rain fell mercilessly upon them, and I swear they sank several inches into the mud as I watched. They stood, heads stuck straight out in front of them (I think in order to maximise water retention along a neck which would normally act as a drain pipe and funnel it all groundwards. This added saturation would thus increase the pathetic effect) with their fleece getting more and more sodden, their little knees buckling slightly, and their backs sagging under the weight. They do actually have a shelter in which to stand, and which I have made all cosy with straw and a net of succulent hay, but they do not use it.

This should actually give me a sense of satisfaction because the shelter was erected by Nic and Kester last autumn because Nic was convinced Dylan and Monty needed somewhere to hide away from the elements. You see Nic is used to horses. Horses are ridiculously delicate creatures that will keel over and die if they eat too much/too little, get too hot/too cold or too wet/too dry or if the wind comes at them from the wrong direction. I know. I had a horse and couldn't believe how much can go wrong with them. Vets grow rich on their equine patients – how on earth do horses ever manage to survive in the wild?

Alpacas, on the other hand, are used to living in the high Andes. When we think it's blowing an arctic gale and brass monkeys are wandering about looking for welders, the alpacas are thinking "Ah, a cooling breeze, how nice". When it snows, a nostalgic tear twinkles in their eyes as they are reminded of home and imagine they can hear the distant sound of pan pipes on the wind. Rain, however, is a bit different. I don't think they quite get the hang of rain. When it rains – and I'm not at home for them to play the Guilt Card on – they take it as an excuse to lie down and chew the cud for a while and wait for it to go away. But generally speaking, our weather is no big deal to them and, being animals living in constant (if irrational) dread of wolves or condors swooping down on them, they like to be out in the open where they can see what's going on.

So I told Nic and Kester that they were wasting their time building a shelter for the alpacas, but of course Men Know Best and so they spent three weekends building the shelter. I have to admit that it is very nice. It has a high gable to match the house, it has a shingle roof and terracotta ridge mounting. They have painted it a very lovely shade of green and there is a very handy little shelf running along the inside upon which they can sit their beers (the men, that is, not the alpacas, although ……). I think, as Nic is my "significant other" and looking to be getting more significant by the week, it was more an exercise in male bonding than anything else since every time I looked outside the deck chairs were out and they were sucking on beer cans and staring at their handiwork discussing what to do next.

And what did the alpacas think when it was all finished? Well, they ignored it. They wouldn't even look at it. They grazed with their backsides pointed at the shelter. The grass is growing lush and green inside, sheltered as it is from the elements, but the alpacas nibble the shorter stuff outside.

This evening, with the rain still coming down like stair

rods, I'll swear the alpacas purposely stood by the fence where I could see them looking all bedraggled, raindrops dripping off their noses and their huge, liquid eyes staring mournfully at me. I know that the rain doesn't really bother them that much. This is all a ploy to get me to rush out there with a hot mash and chopped carrots, and I have to say that it works nearly every time. Wretched creatures.

Note to self: must see about getting Sandra over here to clip the alpacas. That'll put paid to this pity-me stuff ...... on second thoughts, I suppose then they'll stand at the fence shivering instead. I can't win, really, can I?

The hens too refuse to stay in their nice warm coop, but hang about in a huddle under the conifer tree, fluffing their feathers out in an attempt to dry them, but actually getting even wetter. I don't believe there is any such thing as an intelligent hen.

I'd just settled down with my cup of tea when Kester came into the house with his dog Sophie. There was a lot of scuffling and muted shouting, and when I went to discover what the commotion was all about I found that Kester had decided that now (just before I prepared the evening meal) would be the perfect time for him to clip his dog's hair. I did remonstrate with him and ask why he couldn't do it in his room instead of over here, but all I got was a lot of sighing and eye rolling He then launched into a very lengthy and complicated explanation, using a loud, carefully enunciating tone, but I didn't really understand what the explanation was.

To give him his due, Kester did sweep the kitchen floor after the clipping, but it was left to me to tackle the white dog hair that found its way into the living room, onto cushions (how??) and onto my clothes. I then had to bandage Kester's hand as he had discovered during the clipping operation that Sophie did not like having her ears touched, and in fact resented the whole grooming process itself. I then had to mop up the bloody drips he'd made as he went to the bathroom to wash the wound, and wipe blood off various other unexpected places.

And then there were the puddles and wet towels discarded after her bath. These were also left to me as Kester decided that his hand hurt and that he needed to go and have a lie down after all that hard work.

Went to check my e-mails this evening and found one from my Dad, or Rugg as we affectionately call him.

It is a picture of him in a hat.

I'm not quite sure what I'm supposed to read into that. Perhaps nothing. It is just Rugg. He is one of those vaguely dithering individuals who are such fun when they're not yours. When they are yours you spend your time worrying about them and making sure they don't get into trouble, and failing miserably. There was that memorable time when we went shopping with him in a big department store in town. After wandering about the counters I came face to face with Ann, alone. She looked at me with as much surprise as I looked at her.

"Where's Rugg?" she asked.

"I thought he was with you," I said.

At that moment we both spotted him, strolling casually down one of the aisles. He was wearing a rucksack and it was evident that he had taken a stroll (heaven alone knows why. We weren't going to ask) through the ladies' lingerie department because hooked onto his rucksack was a pair of bright red ladies' knickers. They must have kept fluttering so that he would catch sight of them out of the corner of his eye and whirl round to see what was signalling him. But of course the knickers moved as he moved and so were out of sight by the time he turned. So we watched in bemusement as Rugg continued his stroll, every now and again suddenly turning to left or right, trying to catch sight of whatever the elusive thing was that was following him.

Ann and I were both extremely relieved when Rugg, a widower, re-married five years ago. His new wife, Marie, was quite baffled by our unbridled enthusiasm at the announcement of their marriage and the unreserved way we instantly welcomed her into the bosom of our family. Don't get me wrong, Marie in her own right is a lovely person. But by far her best feature is that she now looks after Rugg. And both Ann and I wish her all the luck in the world.

I'm sure we'll miss Rugg when he's gone. Except that he probably won't go. If there is such a thing as the after life Rugg on his death bed would see the beckoning bright light, but wouldn't trust it. Or he'd get lost on the way to it. Or he'd take so long faffing about getting his things together (I know we wouldn't be able to take any "things" with us, but Rugg wouldn't know that and would faff anyway, convinced that there must to *something* he had to pack) that St Peter would get fed up and switch off the light and go to bed. And so Rugg would be doomed to roam the Earth like a lost soul, a sigh on the wind, a strange, vague message on the ether and an interference on the television screen. Haunting us.

So, not much change there then.

Got the briefest of e-mails from Ann today.

"Greetings Grot Bag!" (*Why do I look forward to these missives so much? All I get is verbal abuse and rubbish*)

"Just had a thought (as you do): If fratricide is abridging one's brother, what is the word for bundling one's sister into the canal with her trendy concrete stilettos?

Soeicide?

Sounds too much like suicide to me. In which case, should I commit it, or encourage you to commit it? Such a quandary.

Seeya swoon
Mowl"

See what I mean? – And what are these sudden thoughts about having me fitted for concrete stilettos, or possibly boots? Have I upset her in some way? And should I be worried?

Chapter Three

Disaster! – we had a fox attack last night and lost all but one of our hens. Somehow the wretched creature managed to break into the hen house, and when the girls made a run for it must have chased them because there were feathers all over the garden, and four pathetically mangled bodies. The annoying thing is that the fox didn't take any of the hens away, so it seems it was just an orgy of killing. That, I have discovered since coming to live in the countryside, is Nature for you.

So we have just Attila the Hen left. Either she is traumatised by the events of last night, or she's lonely without her flock because she just hung about under the plum tree all day today and didn't seem inclined to eat or forage. Small was very upset, especially as her own hen, Sister Sarah was killed. Of course the dead hens couldn't just be bagged up and deposited in the bin as I was inclined to do, but Small insisted we had to have a little ceremony and bid a dignified farewell to them all. I have to say, though, that standing over a mass grave, even if it was only slaughtered hens, made me feel a little uneasy, but we got through it. After the eulogy (given by me – and I have to say I found it remarkably difficult to find something apposite and dignified to say about each individual hen, but a glaring Small would not let me get away with a blanket oration) Small tossed a flower onto the little bodies, Kester set to work with the shovel, and then we all went inside to have a cup of tea and a slice of cake.

Roast chicken is off the menu for the rest of the week as a mark of respect.

Comforted Small by telling her that we would get some more hens. I think this time, instead of the Rhode Island Reds we had, I'll get hens rescued from one of those awful battery farms. Apparently the farmers change stock every year, and the old hens go for rendering. Seems sad to me that they should meet with such an end after spending their short lives crammed in cages dutifully producing eggs for us. I think I rather like the idea of providing a retirement home for a few. Small liked the idea too, and she began picking out names for them.

Must look up how to go about it on the net.

I fear that my second daughter, Reeb, is becoming just like her grandfather, the estimable Rugg. She always has been a quiet little thing with an odd sense of humour and a logic that isn't quite the same as everyone else's. Often when having a conversation with Reeb she will say something that makes me stop and think, and I have to carefully backtrack along the topics we have covered in order to see how she has arrived at the statement she has made. I have to admit that you can always find the logic eventually, but it takes some tracking down. There was the memorable occasion when she told me that at school they had been learning about lion waves that rush inland and kill people, especially in China. I listened, a little bemused, for a while thinking, well, there are Chinese dragons and Chinese lions in their mythology, so maybe it's some sort of story she was thinking about, but Reeb insisted that it wasn't myth, it was true. Then it suddenly occurred to me that actually she was talking about tidal waves. When I suggested that this was so she corrected herself cheerfully saying:

"Oh yes, that's it, not lion waves – tiger waves."

There was the other time when we were looking up at the night sky and the little Reeb, aged about six at the time, looked up into the void and pointed out to me the constellation of O'Sean the Hunter. Again I was puzzled as I had not heard of that one, and I asked where it was situated.

"There," she said, pointing again. "You can see his belt."

"Er," I asked hesitantly (I often find myself saying things hesitantly when I'm talking to Reeb), "isn't that Orion's belt?"

"Oh yes," agreed Reeb, "silly me, it's O'Ryan, not O'Sean."

Her confusion (or logic) occurring because our neighbours have two sons called Ryan and Sean. (You do see it, don't you?)

Reeb is currently at college studying beauty therapy. Jay (number one daughter), is already a qualified beauty therapist (why aren't we allowed to say "beauticians" any more??) and she asked Reeb to look after a couple of her clients while she was away on holiday the other week. Today Jay – looking disgustingly tanned and healthy – came round and asked how Reeb had got on. Reeb replied that it had all gone very well, except that she'd had a bit of a problem with Colin. Colin is a sixty-something man who has suffered a number of strokes which have left his fingernails in such a state that he has to have a manicure every two weeks because they flake, discolour and generally drop off if he doesn't. And Colin is a very fastidious person.

"So what about Colin?" asked Jay, nervously.

"Well," explained Reeb, "I was applying a little bit of toilet paper to his nails the other day ......"

"Er, pardon?" interrupted Jay. "Toilet paper?"

"Yes, his nail had split right down and I was putting toilet paper over the split, then I went to add the superglue – "

"Toilet paper and superglue?" asked Jay faintly.

"Yes," said the unmoved Reeb, "that's how you repair split nails."

"No," said Jay, very carefully, "you apply a silk wrap and acrylic to my clients – especially Colin!"

"But I didn't have any silk wraps," said Reeb, "so I improvised. Anyway, it was OK except that when I went to take the lid off the superglue it was stuck, and so I had to use my teeth, and when it finally did come off, the superglue burst in my mouth and I got my lips and hair stuck to the lid, and when I went to pull it off I got glue on my hands, the toilet paper, Colin's hands, Colin's shirt and the table. It was a bit tricky to get everything separated."

Jay blinked owlishly.

"But you did get it sorted?" she asked.

"Oh yes," said the little Reeb. "Luckily Colin's wife Gillian had some solvent, and she said she never did like the table anyway."

"And how did Colin take it all?" asked Jay faintly.

Reeb shrugged dismissively, "I just told him it happened all the time, and he was all right about it."

The horrifying thing is that it probably does happen all the time to Reeb. No one else. Just Reeb!

I had planned that we should have a barbeque today, as yesterday was so lovely and sunny. Since this afternoon the weather changed this now meant that we all sat inside watching through the windows as the Stoic Reeb sat outside in the howling gale hunched under a battered umbrella over a very smoky fire waiting until the meat was sufficiently warm as to count as being cooked. Then we all helped ourselves to outwardly blackened, pink-centred sausages and kebabs, and made appreciative yummy noises in the direction of the faintly steaming, hickory-smoked Reeb before passing it under the table to the waiting dogs and trying to pig out on salad and garlic bread.

Of course it would have been far more sensible to abandon the idea of a barbeque for the day and cook everything up in the kitchen, but since when have we ever been sensible?

After the lovely sunshine we had recently, it is now chilly. I mentioned to Ann the fact that our office is particularly cold at the moment, and for some obscure reason she suggested that I could always set fire to my socks to keep warm. No doubt she thought she was offering a kindly suggestion, but I felt that setting fire to my socks would be but a short term solution – entertaining, and possibly awe inspiring, though it may be with the sudden flash and flare that would undoubtedly occur given the amount of highly inflammable deodorant that lingers down there. But, no, although I did ponder the option I then thought that setting fire to the building would be much better. Not only would I have the cosy warmth now, but long-term I would get to stay home in decadent idleness, put my feet up on the mantle and spit at the ceiling for a while. The alpacas are obviously rubbing off on me – filthy beasts! ...... Now how can I get lanolin out of clothes?

Was glad to get an e-mail from Ann this evening.

"Wotcha Fish Face" – *it's refreshing to see that the loving respect continues* –

"Don't you just love the modern way of speaking? Much of it designed by management to wind up lesser mortals, like those people in the accounts department (sorry, finance department) with high-faluting pretentious verbiage! (Guess where I work?) Apparently we no longer have jobs, we *define our roles*. Gone is the good old admin and personnel, we now have logistics and human resources, who, no doubt, work twenty-four seven (--!!***).

OK, so I'm Rugg's daughter" (*there's a bold and unexpected admission, I thought*) "and I don't go with all this modern talk. I work in a good old-fashioned *accounts office*. So you can see right away that we have a clash of cultures. So there we are, accounts office completely bogged down with year-end, month-end, auditors and general catch-up just wanting to be left alone to get on with their work. Bright Young Up-and-Comer (in accounts-speak – smart Alec!) breezes into the office and announces that everyone in the company must go on a team-building course.

Yeah, right.

There were e-mails and spreadsheets (and probably power

point presentations) that had been circulating outlining who, what, when and where. Apparently. We didn't see this in accounts. We had our heads down. Don't know where they all went.

Then, one day, Helen disappeared. We noticed this as no one went to fetch the tea at 10.30am. Then, next day, she came back mumbling and muttering something about 'a complete and utter waste of time'. Disturbing, but incomprehensible comment duly noted. Heads back down. Next day the boss comes up to my desk, peers over all the paperwork stacked up on it and says: 'Ann, you've got to go on a one-day course. Pauline was supposed to go, but she has flatly refused' (Pauline is also a parish counsellor, so when she refuses, she stays refused!) 'We all have to go sooner or later,' continued the boss, 'so will you go? Tomorrow?'

Wot? I found out – from Helen – where to go and what time and what to wear.

So the next day I turn up at the 'Learning Island'. I.e., the office right at the farthest end of the mezzanine floor in the factory! No beach, no palm trees, no iced drinks, no reggae music …… no lights and no people!

Check with boss that we do have the correct day. Yes, just stay there, someone is sure to be along in a minute. Lurk about in dark corridor. Eventually mooch back to office. Meet the Training Officer – note, I did say the *Training Officer*. Yes, he says, go back to the 'Learning Island', it's all OK.

Lurk, lurk.

Then up comes the cleaning lady – note, I did say the *cleaning lady*.

'Are you all right, dear?' she asks.

'Yes,' I reply, 'just waiting for my training course.'

'Oh, that's not until tomorrow, luv.'

!!!!@@@*****

Well, who would you believe? Yes, so did I. And duly went back to my office to wait until the course started the next day.

As for the course itself. Well! – team building, my left

earlobe! It was showing us all how 'Lean Manufacturing' works, which is suspicious in itself. I thought 'Lean Manufacturing' was all about employing thin people. Now I know better.

We set up a mini factory with all the relevant departments (including finance/accounts), a customer and a supplier. Then we made (to order) lots of twee little metal boxes and showed how profitable we could be. We were then made progressively leaner until we were running as sweetly as a well-oiled machine. Hmmmmm.

OK, I suppose there was some team building in a sense. In the sense that each of us was given a role (job) that they did not usually do (so you got some, but not much, idea of what other people did). OK, in theory, but I don't get the point of teaching us how smoothly a factory can run in lean mode when you have pen-pushers on the line and factory workers in the office!

How smoothly can it run?

Picture the scene: we had a welder in stores. The customer was an engineer and various bods who are normally on the factory assembly lines were in sales and finance (accounts) and – wait for it – a Mowl, complete with an electric screwdriver, armed and dangerous on Assembly Line One!!! I took bets on how soon we could get the organiser (-?) to run screaming from the room, lips foaming!

Well, I was lean. I was keen. I had no end of fun arranging my little boxes of screws and washers and bits into the ideal order and went at it great guns. Had a little party, I did. But then, I am a woman. Lean manufacturing is all about common sense. Putting things in a logical order so as not to waste time. Do not use superfluous forms (and staff). Well, as I said, we are women. What other way is there to run your household, and especially your kitchen? What, we asked (the accounts department is all women) is all the fuss about? The factory, however, is run by men. Enough said. Well, it was great fun, but wot a waste of time!

Still, I do get a certificate. Muted jubilation.

I did cause some hilarity during the proceedings. The chaps surged round to see a woman (and a pen-pusher at that) using an electric drill. The drill failed to work straight off and was dangling from a wire on my work station (table to you), so I assumed that I had to switch the electricity on by means of this pull cord ...... then some helpful chap – having straightened up from laughing – informed me that 'you can't get the drill to work by switching on the light, you know!' Drat. Sussed. Didn't know I was being watched. And yes, it was a *battery* drill! Shame! Blush! And yes, Lam was terrified by the prospect of a fully-certificated drill-conversant Mowl.

Be warned. Be very afraid.

Well me old Fruit, must go now – must drill out some accounts.

Love twall
Mowl

PS: We are supposed to leave a message on our voice mail and I had a couple of thoughts:

You're talking to Ann from Saltash
Who ran off to the loo in a dash
It may well be true
That I'm not on the loo
But to the tell you the truth would be rash

Or

I'm sorry I'm not here for you
But I had to run off to the loo.
I thought I'd be brief
But found to my grief
That I ended up having a poo!

Finally settled on:

I'm sorry that I was away
When you called and had something to say.
Leave your name, number too
And I'll get back to you
Thanks for calling – and have a nice day!

Funnily enough my boss didn't like any of them. No soul,
some people."

The thought of my sister being a certified lean, keen,
drilling machine is certainly something to muse upon.

I shall say nothing about her lyrical attempts. Some people
ought to have their poetic licence revoked and receive severe
punishment for inflicting bad poetry upon an unsuspecting
audience. Something lingering, like being made to submit
to a ducking stool followed by a slow roasting over a gentle
flame.

That would teach them.

Chapter Four

Got the opportunity to take a break in Center Parcs for a long weekend. Center Parcs is a holiday village with little chalets nestled in woodland, lakes to admire, a huge "tropical" indoor swimming pool, and various outdoor activities to enjoy. It is really the English equivalent of an American "dude ranch", except that you don't break horses or ride bulls, or do any roping, tying or branding, or eat beans round a camp fire ..... so not really anything like a dude ranch at all, come to think about it.

But you know what I mean - it's designed for townies who rarely venture into the countryside and so are enchanted by the (neatly kept) forests and lakes and delighted at having the wildlife right on their doorstep. And, like a Disney film, the wildlife knows its lines and acts accordingly. Every morning we had a duck come waddling up to the patio doors and knock with its bill, waiting hopefully for bread. We had geese strolling passed at regular intervals (rather too regular, I thought. I had this suspicion that just stage left was a man with a cage who let them out, then, when they'd waddled obligingly passed our windows, they were captured by an accomplice with another cage, then moved on to the next villa), and squirrels doing unspeakable things (it is spring - ahem!) in the treetops and, more startlingly, on our barbeque. Had to draw the curtains and suddenly talk

about other things as a wide-eyed Small opened her mouth
to ask what I knew would be embarrassing questions.

The only trouble with Center Parcs is that it's a bit
herdish, if you know what I mean. There are a lot of people
there, so you have to be smiley and polite all the time, and
you are expected to join in things. And be jolly. I don't
do jolly. There is also a lot of camaraderie. I don't do
camaraderie either. Nor bon homme. Bah humbug I can
just about summon up. I managed to survive by communing
with nature and for the most part ignoring the humanity (oh
the humanity!) around me.

For all that we had a good time. Small loved it, of course,
which is really why we went.

While we were there I began thinking about Rugg and
Marie because I've been a bit worried about them recently.
They are both in their 80's now and getting rather frail, and
I thought that they could do with a little relaxing break, so
wondered if Center Parcs would be a suitable place to bring
them for a long weekend. Because of this I looked around
the place with new eyes, trying to imagine them there. Felt
that they could well appreciate the huge domed "paradise"
swimming pool. It is done out in a Balinese theme with
tropical plants and island statuary with plenty of places to
sit, have a drink and people watch. They could even swim
if they felt so inclined, or maybe join in some of the more
energetic activities.

Once I got into the swing of it I could really see Rugg and
Marie backstroking through the water, whizzing down the
flumes, and I would give an awful lot of money to see them
both tackle the "white water rapids". This is a current of
water that swirls round the outside of the dome, bumping
over ridges, rushing round corners and creating foaming
cascades of water that twirl you about, slam you into walls
and finally deposits you, turd-like, into a swirling toilet bowl
at the end. It is great fun. But I believe the greatest fun is
had by Small Children who shall remain nameless (Emma-
Lee!) watching their mother being dunked, spun, battered,

tangled with complete strangers and finally tipped headfirst, feet skyward with no dignity whatsoever into the final pool.

It soothed my battered ego to imagine my father, who gives a whole new meaning to the word phlegmatic, being thus manhandled, and even raised a smile (a sort of "kick the cat" satisfaction).

I could also imagine (I was really getting into my reverie by now) Rugg and Marie on a tandem sailing through the woodlands, avoiding erotically tangled squirrels and tinkling their bicycle bells merrily as they unwittingly tipped other cyclists into a ditch. And then there is the zip wire ...... I could just see Rugg being strapped into a harness, hooked to a wire seventy feet up in a tree, then being pushed off to rush along the wire on a long sloping trajectory groundwards. It seems very "him", I think. Just the thought of taking him there, explaining what was going to happen to him, and then watching his jaw work as various comments passed through his mind gives me a lot of joy.

I worry about myself sometimes.

Small and I went canoeing – and I got soaked. Small didn't, I did. I don't know how this works, but everything we do she ends up hooting at me because I get into some kind of predicament. We were in a two person canoe, each with our own compartments. My compartment, the front one, had holes in it. I thought this was a fault, but when I looked in other canoes, they had them too. So apparently they were supposed to be there, but I cannot think why unless it is solely to afford amusement to the person sitting behind. Within a very short space of time I was sitting in a small pool of water, which was bad enough, but then every time I lifted my paddle the water ran down the handle and deposited itself into my lap, so I was getting wet from two directions, and then, every now and again, my paddle (or it could be Small's – I have suspicions on this score) would scoop up water and slap it onto the back of my head to trickle coldly down my back.

Emerged from the canoe after our half hour just as wet as if I had taken a dive into the lake! Cycled squelchingly back to the villa for a change of clothes and a comforting mug of hot chocolate.

But all in all it was Fun. Felt quite invigorated (which is a euphemism for exhausted) and ready for the mundanety of ornery life when we left.

Back home I have to say that the garden was looking very nice. The cherry trees and apple trees were full of blossom, and I was particularly pleased to see that quite a few of the daffodils I had planted in the autumn had actually come up and were flowering. It was all very cheering. I admired the flowers for all of two days. Then, feeling sorry for the alpacas because their field is chewed away to nothing, I let them out to gorge on the beautiful lush green grass of the lawn for a while. However, they decided to have a side salad of daffs, and now all I have is a host – a crowd (if you will) of verdant stalks. Funny how alpacas don't eat nettles. We have plenty of nettles, but they ignore them.

Wrathfully I chased Dylan and Monty back into their paddock, where they quite unrepentantly stretched their necks over the fence and began nibbling at the new magnolia tree I had just planted. I thought I had put it well out of their reach, but I did not realise that alpacas could well be a cross between a sheep, a camel and a giraffe. One of Nature's little orgies in the dim and distant past, I suspect. Darwin could have written a whole book about them. I think it's just another example of God's sense of humour and a way of keeping Man in his place. As I have remarked before: Dominion over the animals – yeah, right!

I don't know, what with the alpacas gorging on my daffs and magnolia, and the starlings decimating the crocuses that dared peep up through the grass, I sometimes wonder why I bother!

I'm not turning into a Grumpy Old Woman, am I? Oo er.

Talking of Grumpy Old Women, I received an e-mail from Ann.

"Wotcha Old Boot Face!" (*Thinks: is it better to be called an Old Boot, or to have your face compared to one? I'm not sure there's much difference, and either way there is abuse involved. I must have a word with my sister*)

"We snuck off to Dartmouth on Saturday. Took the pretty way through Kingsbridge then through Start Bay where the road is a narrow strip of land between the nature reserve lake and the sea. Stopped off to look at all the wild birds, but they assumed we had some bread and went and fetched each other from all the surrounding tussocks and swarmed up to honk at us expectantly. It all got very noisy, and just a little threatening, so we backed off and drove away.

Looked for a place to get some refreshments and found a lovely little tea shop overlooking the sea. Settled into our seats at a window table and put in our order for a cheeseburger (for Lam) and a toasted teacake (for me), plus a pot of tea. It was ten past four and we were informed by the waitress that they closed at five o'clock, and so had stopped serving food ......!

Only in the depths of the South West.

Went on to some shops – which were fortunately still prepared to serve us, despite the advanced hour. Your mention of doing a jig saw puzzle the other week got me going, so I bought a Monet and cut it up into little pieces – no! – I bought a Monet jig saw puzzle from a charity shop (£1.25, my life, already!) and took it home. That very evening I settled down, a little music in the background, a glass of wine to hand, and began putting it together. Some while later Lam came into the room and eyed it askance. He has never seen me do a jig saw puzzle before. He does not understand. I use a rasp and a hammer. It works very well. The sky goes together beautifully, except that it does tend to bow out in the middle, and I keep having to push at it or apply the hammer. Enter (as I said) the Lam and, eyes popping out and hair on end, he cries:

'What have you done?'

And proceeds to rip about two thirds of my hard work out and re-arrange it.

How mean! It looked perfect to me. I must admit, though, that it was a bit flatter his way, and I was no longer stuck for the next piece. I shall persist.

I have been giving some considerable thought to your alpaca problem, and I have a theory. *Enter soap box, padded shoulder jacket, nose in air and finger pointing decisively – though, knowing my luck, it will be pointing decisively up my trunk!* I believe that you have failed to assert yourself. You must (enter clip board) be first in everything. You must kick harder, spit further, eat more daffodils and ignore more nettles than they do! Your wig should be wilder and your fleece softer. I recommend that Ole Stinky be hoiked back from the Antipodes (or wherever he is sojourning at the moment) to help you in the spitting department. I just feel it in my bones that a spit from Ole Stinky would level all opposition. Then all you will have to do is appear at the entrance of the field, brandish your castrating irons and shout –

'Oi! You two! Pack that in!'

Then they will be sure to stop whatever it is they are not supposed to be doing, indeed, they will be putty in your hands.

And having shared my wisdom with you (an invoice will be in the post), I shall bid you adieu.

Mowl."

Ann is wrong in her assumption that I need Stinky's help in this matter. I can spit further than an alpaca. Years of practise and horrified kids, my dear. This may, of course, be seen as a Bad Example. I don't care. I decided long ago that being kind to the children and trying to be a Good Mother was never going to work. Everybody knows that all mental instabilities and deviancies, without exception, can be blamed on the Mother and how she influenced young childhood. If she was a Negligent Mother, naturally everyone could purse their lips and frown, knowing exactly what went wrong. If she was the Perfect Mother, on the other hand, she set a standard the child knew it could never reach and therefore crushed their spirit and instilled feelings of inadequacy and anxiety. And Mediocre Mother, trying desperately to walk the tightrope between these two evils, will instead provide a wealth of intriguing and complicated problems from either end of the spectrum for her offspring to call upon.

So I acknowledge that sad reality. Indeed, I embrace it. When the day comes for any of my children to lie on that psychiatrist's couch and lay bare their soul, there will be no need for deep digging or regression hypnosis. Everything I have done to blight their little lives will be there, at the forefront, jubilating, ready to be analysed and corrected.

They can thank me later.

Chapter Five

Nic used to be a commercial airline pilot. That was long before I knew him, but recently he has been struck with the desire to get back into the sky, and, not content with the thought of just hiring a plane every now and again to go for a flight, he decided that he would buy his own. I'm not really quite sure what I imagined when he said he was going to buy a plane, I don't have a great deal of interest in them myself, but the Dornier DO28 STOL aircraft he eventually plumped for somehow surprised me.

Maybe it's the fact that it's rather older than I imagined it would be, or perhaps the fact that it needed quite a lot of work doing to it. I don't know. I just know that I was surprised. And not necessarily in a good way.

Anyway, I'd been able to put it out of my mind for the past few months as it was down at Lee-on-Solent being brought back to airworthiness, but then Nic announced, face beaming, that it was ready for us to fetch it up here. From the eager light in his eye and the way he stared at me as if waiting for an enthusiastic response it occurred to me that the use of the word "us" really did mean us.

"Oh," I said, a little faintly. "Good?"

Nic ignored the query in the final word and gave me a hug.

"I knew you'd be pleased!" Nic declared – he never was very good at body language, facial expressions, subtle hints or in fact anything other than blunt and blatant declarations of intent or feeling. "I've made arrangements for us to go down and collect it this weekend and bring it up to Shuttleworth."

Now I'm not very good at flying. Well, the flying is OK, indeed rather wonderful if you're in a big, substantial jet with full complement of crew and reassuringly smiling stewardesses handing you large glasses of wine, and when you're so far above the clouds that the ground can hardly be seen. But even in a big, substantial jet the take offs and landings are still nerve-wracking for me, as you see the ground falling away from you or coming at you. Which rather leads me to think that the real problem is that of heights, rather than of flying per se. And I wouldn't call it a fear either – more blind, screaming terror. When placed in a situation involving heights, be it on a ladder or a cliff edge, I come out in a sweat, I can't talk, can hardly breath, and my brain goes into a sort of seizure while my whole body trembles with a bizarre urge to jump.

Anyway, Jay drove us down to Lee, parked up the car and waved to us as we walked across the airfield to the hangar where the Dornier was waiting, Nic with a decided skip in his step, me now with leaden feet and a sense of dread sitting lumpenly in the pit of my stomach, raising my heart rate and drying my mouth. I felt that the opening of the hangar doors should have been accompanied by some kind of dramatic, doom-laden music, but sadly it wasn't. There was just a lot of creaking (from the doors and Nic's knees) and the white and red plane was revealed to my gaze.

The airfield at Lee-on-Solent was not what you might call bustling. Apparently the airfield was winding down and companies re-locating, in fact the people who had worked on the Dornier had already gone, and our plane was the last thing left to be removed. Consequently there were no personnel to be seen anywhere, and the hangar where the Dornier resided had a forlorn, deserted air about it. Such surroundings did not enhance the look of the plane which stood amongst the debris of old oil cans, discarded rags and other general paraphernalia looking rather ancient and well-worn.

To Nic, however, it was a thing of beauty, and he walked up to it, touching the wing with a caress that almost made me jealous, and went all around it, checking things out and making little cooing noises of appreciation.

Somehow we had to push the plane out of the hangar. Since it was manifestly too heavy for just us two to do, Nic went off to find somebody, anybody, to help. Left alone with the Dornier I stared at it with misgiving. I walked all around it. I touched the wing, hoping that perhaps with physical contact I might feel something inside of me, I don't know what, but a sensation that might inspire some kind of confidence or at least calm about the coming flight. I peered into the cockpit and stared at all the old dials and switches and noted the torn ceiling lining and worn leather seats, and all the time my heart sank lower and my mouth became drier.

Nic arrived back at the hangar, almost running in his eagerness, with an overalled man in tow. Between us we pushed the Dornier outside, and then a tanker pulled up and fuelling took place. I stood at a distance watching the proceedings as though locked into some kind of dream.

When all the fuelling and checks had been completed Nic turned to me.

"Are you sure you want to do this?" he asked.

"NO!!" screamed my brain; "Yes," said my loyal tongue.

"You don't have to," Nic said in a kindly tone, "I won't be offended if you don't come this time. Jay is still there, waiting to see us take off, so you could always go back home with her if you wanted."

My tongue was now cleaving to the roof of my mouth, so I smiled weakly and gargled something incoherent which Nic took to be confirmation of my first statement.

We climbed into the cockpit. It is very cramped. It is very old. It is (not very reassuringly) called a clockwork cockpit. Things don't work. I was strapped in. A wise move since my hand had located the door handle and my brain was insisting that an escape could be made, even at 3,000 feet. Then we went through pre-flight checks. I have to say that my gently bubbling panic was not helped by the sight of Nic studying dials in a frowning (dare I say slightly puzzled) way and saying things like:

"So where's the altimeter? Ah, yes. And this must be the auxiliary generator switch I suppose."

I SUPPOSE??!!

The full impact of the fact that this was the first time Nic had ever flown this plane alone then hit me and I sat rigidly, swallowing hard and wondering if I'd told the children what bank accounts I have and where the water stop cock in the kitchen is located (don't ask. I don't know why that's important in the face of possible imminent death, but apparently it is). There was a bit more tweaking, surprised exclamations and switch flicking, and then Nic decided we were ready to go.

It was as we were rolling towards the runway and he was trying to inform those who ought to know that G-ASUR was about to take off that Nic discovered the radio didn't work.

"Never mind," he said cheerily as we roared down the runway and I clamped my eyes tight shut and clung with all my strength to the edge of my seat, "I've got a hand held back up radio."

And then, as we soared to 3,000 feet and the Solent stretched glistening beneath us with the Isle of Wight on our starboard side –

"Ah, that doesn't seem to be working either."

So there we were, strapped into an ancient aeroplane heading north into bad weather with no radio. Terrific, I thought, nervously eyeing the black clouds, the options for death have just multiplied. What fun.

I have to say that after a few minutes my panic abated

to manageable proportions and I was able to appreciate the view from the Dornier. England looks so beautiful, still very green and rural, the towns looking neat and compact nestled in the bosom of nature rather than overshadowing it. Strangely (and most relieving for a grateful Pherrit) our flight path took us down canyons of piling clouds much of the time, rather than through them. When we did go through the cloud it was not as bumpy as it could have been, and I coped quite well. It did rain, which was another thing that worried me as the Dornier has no de-icing capability, but since we were below 10,000 feet the icing was not critical. However, I can tell you that the Dornier leaks, so I was kept busy trying to keep the map dry (no hope for myself).

So about forty-five minutes into the flight, my terror dropping back to mid-range anxiety, a voice beside me says with quiet vehemence:

"Oh, sh-sh-sh-sugar."

And then silence.

Now I can tell you that a nervous passenger does not want to hear the pilot utter an expletive. A terrified passenger *certainly* does not want to hear this, and particularly does not want it followed by silence! The mid-range anxiety ramped up to full blown alarm and a blackness swam before my eyes. After several desperate swallows I managed to ask, as diffidently as I could:

"Um, is there a problem?"

"Yes," replied Nic tersely.

Terse is also not how one wants ones pilot to talk, and an uncompromising "yes" to a query about danger is also totally unwanted.

Another silence.

A bit more swallowing. Desperate attempt then to get some kind of lubrication into the mouth to allow speech.

"Um, what sort of problem?" I enquire, trying to sound casual. "I mean, is it a particularly dangerous one?"

Hand now firmly on the door catch.

"No, it's OK." But Nic's voice did not sound reassuring.

I glared at the props and cocked my head to try to discern any change in engine sound.

"Are we going to be all right?" my voice was now very faint.

"Oh yes," Nic's voice was now back to normal and the frown had gone. "I think we might have gone into somebody's air space, that's all, because of the lack of radio. But we're unidentified, so it'll be all right."

The flight lasted ninety minutes, and for me it was ninety minutes of unremitting fear, troughing and peaking between apprehension and blind terror, which is absolutely exhausting. By the time we located Milton Keynes and then Cranfield I was ready to land. We flew over Cardington hangars and looked for Old Warden, but it is nestled in trees and proved to be elusive. We flew around, scouring the ground below, and then Nic had to go back to Cranfield and approach again – and again we couldn't find it. By now my panic was almost overwhelming, not helped by the fact that to look for Old Warden Nic was standing the Dornier on it's wing tips for a better view. My brain was screaming:

"Just put down at Cranfield! Just put down at Cranfield! – I'll call Kester for a lift home."

And then he spotted the airfield, and we came down. We touched down onto wet grass, and to the delectation of the few onlookers shot along the runway and then did what seemed to me to be a nifty handbrake turn so that we were suddenly facing in the opposite direction.

"Neat," I thought, "stops us overshooting the runway on damp grass, that manoeuvre."

Then I noticed that Nic's face had a surprised expression on it and apparently he had just discovered that one of the brakes was working better than the other, hence the spin – not a manoeuvre at all!

I unstrapped and wobbled away from the Dornier desperately desiring a good shot of whiskey or brandy, but having to make do with the Shuttleworth café coffee. Nic, meanwhile, went up again with his mate John at the controls to show him how best to approach Old Warden and how to stop gracefully, so that he'll know better next time.

Next time – ha!

Was glad to get home and went straight to my computer hoping that there would be something from Ann to cheer me up.

"Greetings O Skin and Blister!" (*I felt better already*)

"I have gone off bacon. Bacon may smell and taste nice, but it has some rude habits. Like spitting. Specifically, like spitting hot fat at poor unsuspecting Mowls. The rasher in question aimed a particularly nasty fat-spit directly at my thumb and I had to retreat and place said digit under the cold tap for a while. I thought no more about it – until, of course, I did some gardening and introduced rose bushes to sore thumb. That night said thumb blistered up and next morning (early) blister got caught on something.

One Mowl instantly wide-awake.

One thumb looking decidedly nasty.

One Mowl prostrate on bed thinking,

'I can't faint over such a silly thing as this!'

No? Just for once the lie down sorted out the faint – I have the capacity of fainting even when horizontal and I had laid back down on the bed just so as to give myself the benefit of a soft place to 'get it over with', but there you go.

Woke up Lam for some sympathy and go get him to fetch plasters, gauze and scissors in order for the gory digit to be mopped up and covered up. Lam unrolled about a mile of gauze and considered wrapping it about one hundred times around the thumb, fingers, hand and on up the arm (possibly to cover the mouth as well since he was getting decidedly irritated by both my squeals and instructions). However, following some discussion he curtailed his artistic talents to just a bound up thumb and a bit of sticking plaster.

OK. Great.

Now I had to go downstairs to clear up the kitchen, and then negotiate a shower. Decided that a rubber glove would be handy (ha ha), and then, being a positive thinking sort of person, I decided that all this presented an Opportunity for scientific experimentation.

How much can a Mowl do with her left paw, and how much can be (successfully) achieved in a rubber glove. I would here like to state that this epistle is not a cheap bid for sympathy, which I know I would not get from my sister anyway – more a lot of chortling and gloating, I suspect – but the sharing of a truly scientific experiment.

My findings are as follows:

1. Given the alternative (Lam washing up) Lams definitely approve of Mowls using dishwashers midweek.

2. The buttering of toast left-handed is more difficult than would be supposed and is an exercise in frustration v science.

3. Left-handed excursions into large (and almost empty) jam pots lead to a sticky end (very enjoyable).

4. The kettle faces the wrong way.

5. Hot water splashed on burns = ouch!

6. In the Science v Frustration stakes, science loses hands (thumbs) down.

Showering in a rubber glove is also an interesting pastime. Rubber gloves are really only of use while the arm is extended in the upright position, or if the water is shallow. Position it downwards, in deep or running water, and the water gleefully races down the arm to fill up said glove and swish around in gay abandon producing soggy and indescribable organic soup in little finger from which evolve creatures which can only be found in the book of Revelation. Also, lathering soap over ones body using a rubber glove feels decidedly weird. Helen at work said: 'Isn't that what husbands are for?' Lam approves of that suggestion. Following on from that I discovered that you can aim a bar of soap at your husband just as easily with a rubber glove as without. Possibly better.

And then there's the small matter of going to the loo …… don't go there! – Well, yes, OK, you can go to the loo, but – and this is a very big butt – I think that this part of the experiment should pass into the realms of myth and legend and your more than adequate imagination.

Apart from that, everything else seems much as usual.

Love twall
Mowl"

I felt a little soothed by this tale of woe. But not much.

Chapter Six

I decided to treat our dog Arfer to a beautiful big, juicy bone the other day. Arfer is called Arfer because he is 'alf a rottweiler and 'alf German shepherd. Kester named him. I distance myself from the appellation.

I gave Arfer the bone out in the garden, after all I did not want any yucky, greasy muck over the furniture and carpets. He seemed delighted. But a few minutes later, it had vanished. Arfer was lying with his huge head resting on his paws under the apple tree, but of the bone there was no sign.

Small and I looked for it, but to no avail. I was a bit peeved that Arfer had managed to lose it so quickly, I had thought he would be able to enjoy it for several hours, if not days. So the next day I sent Reeb out to buy him another one. I felt Arfer needed a bone that particular day as we were expecting visitors and, since he takes his guarding duties extremely seriously, I have to keep Arfer tied up when people come, and a nice juicy bone would keep him happy and occupied.

So I handed Arfer his second bone and he stood, holding his thigh of cow in his mouth not quite knowing what to do with it. After a few minutes contemplation he began pacing, which is quite hard to do when you are tied to a tree. The upshot was that he plodded round and round and round – until at last he was bang up against the tree trunk with nowhere else to go. After a moment's thought he turned round and plodded back the other way, bone still firmly gripped in mouth, until the rope was all played out ...... then he turned round and walked the other way. I watched in fascination as he did this several times. Finally he settled down on the grass with the bone on his paws, cuddling it rather than chewing it.

After our visitors had left, I let Arfer off the lead and he picked up his bone and promptly vanished. After a while I became a little concerned and went looking for him. There was no sign of him on the lawns, back or front. I searched the paddock and inside the alpaca shelter, but to no avail. Eventually, after much calling a black and tan face peeped furtively out from the bushes at the front of the house, then disappeared. Curious, I went to the bush and peered in. Arfer was busy burying his bone – not with his paws, oh no. He was shovelling dirt and leaves over it with his face! I left him to it.

He came in eventually and, after a bit of shouting on my part, and vigorous application with a brush and towel in order to save my kitchen floor becoming too grime-besmeared, I gave him his dinner. Reeb, thinking that he would be too engrossed with his meal to notice her leaving, went out to see how the bone burial had gone. But Arfer wasn't to be so duped. He immediately left his food and went out after her. When he found that his hiding place had been discovered, Arfer shot Reeb a reproachful look, retrieved Sean (by this time I had named the bone Sean of the Dead since it had received a decent burial, but was apparently intent on coming back) and tried to bring it into the house. There was a bit of shouting – well, I shouted and Arfer just stood in the porch looking at me, Sean in a vile dirt and leaf covered state gripped firmly in his jaws, and finally I let him bring it inside, only because he wouldn't let go of the thing and I couldn't persuade anybody else to touch it to take it away from him. Unusually, Arfer wanted to stay downstairs that night instead of coming up to our bedroom to sleep.

Ah, the love of a dog for his bit of rotting cow skeleton!

Anyway, that night I lay in bed in the darkness waiting in trepidation for the sounds of Sean dragging his bloody, ragged fleshed self up the stairs, and then the rattle of the door handle as he crept into the bedroom. The room was bathed in pearly moonlight, but I just knew that a bank of black clouds would scud across the sky and obscure the moon just as the eerie shape leaned over the bed to smother me with my own pillow as I lay paralysed with fear ......

Nic told me not to be so stupid and go to sleep.

Next day Arfer and Sean sat out in the garden together enjoying the sunshine, and I noticed that Arfer kept cocking his head as though listening to something. Perhaps it was the voice of Sean whispering to him.

"What's that you say, Sean? – Kill them, kill them all? No, Sean, I couldn't. That would be wrong ...... "

And then Sean vanished, presumably buried in some more secluded part of the garden, perhaps alongside the first Sean. I'm keeping a close eye on Arfer now, and if he and the cat get out the Ouija board in order to communicate with Sean, I shall start to worry!

Whilst on the subject of animals, I noticed that the toenails of one of our alpacas, Monty, were getting rather long and curling round onto each other, so Reeb and I decided we needed to do something about them. Reeb and I have worked out quite a good routine for corralling the alpacas, a routine that was devised in order to stop the frustration of chasing two long-legged, swift-footed and devious creatures round and round a field for hours on end. We use a long pole which we hold between us, and then hold sticks in our other hands so that we form a long barrier as we approach the alpacas. By advancing slowly we can get them penned into a corner, or even their shed if we're lucky, and then one person can take hold of the pole and take the role of Wall whilst the other lucky person captures one of the alpacas. Once you've caught one, you've effectively got them both since they do not like to be far away from one another.

So we managed to pen the boys into their shed without too much problem, and then we allowed Dylan out so that we had Monty on his own. Unfortunately Monty became quite agitated when he saw Dylan out in the field away from him, so Reeb and I began making soothing noises as we moved in to take hold of Monty and tried to persuade him to lie down. Monty, however, was having none of it, and the gentle persuasion turned into a wrestling match. Reeb clung desperately to the halter rope whilst I tried to grab hold of a prancing, dancing alpaca and pull his legs from under him. He leaped and skittered like a thing possessed, and I got kicked for my pains. Fortunately a kick from an alpaca is not as bad as it sounds since they have small, cushiony feet, making a kick from one of them rather like a soft punch. But whilst the kicking wasn't so bad, the spitting was another matter, and both Reeb and I were liberally sprayed with alpaca spittle from both Monty and Dylan who was hovering nearby watching what we were doing to his mate ...... tell me again, why did I think owning alpacas was a good idea??

Eventually we put hay bales in front of the shelter in order to barricade Monty inside, and then we retreated to wipe off the alpaca spit and confer. Once I'd got my breath back we returned to the fray. We tried leaning on Monty's back, pushing him down with all our might, and this time his knees did buckle, and with a bad tempered grumbling groan and one last defiant spit, he reluctantly lay down. But upright, if you see what I mean, tucking his legs firmly beneath his body. More brute force as I tried to push him over onto his side, but he kept rolling back up. Finally, with an almighty heave, I managed it, his legs appeared from beneath him, and Reeb knelt gently on his neck to keep him still. I know that might sound horrendous, but honestly, that is what you do to stop them thrashing about and hurting themselves.

Somewhat flushed and panting hard, I was just fetching out the secateurs (yes, garden secateurs – there's nothing subtle about an alpaca pedicure!) when Dylan came up behind Reeb, reached over her shoulder and grabbed Monty by an ankle with his teeth, and began pulling! – Screams as we thought he might actually bite Monty's foot off he was gripping so hard, and there was a decidedly manic look in his eye. But then he gave a final heave and flipped Monty over, out of Reeb's grip and up onto his feet so that he could escape! Couldn't believe it!

The alpacas retreated triumphantly and stood in a huddle (can you have a huddle of two?), watching us.

More discussion between Reeb and me, and then we decided to call in reinforcements. I penned Monty into the shed again whilst Reeb went and fetched Kester. Now Kester is not awfully keen on dealing with animals, especially not when kicking, mud and spit are involved. He came stumping out, hands firmly thrust into pockets and with hunched shoulders which declared to all interested parties that he was here under sufferance, only because his Mother demanded it, and at the first opportunity he was heading back to his shed where he would firmly draw the curtains against the bucolic idyll that lurked outside his windows, and turn up his music very loud. However, we persuaded him that he did not need to get fully involved in the operation and that all he had to do was keep Dylan at bay whilst we tended to Monty, and he finally agreed. In fact he became unexpectedly enthusiastic.

I have already mentioned that Kester is an engineering apprentice, he is also a bit of a tinkerer with all things mechanical. He has been working for some months on something which the rest of the family refer to as the Diabolical Machine. It lives under a blanket in a section of the barn behind a locked door. It might be a turbine. We're not sure. It is noisy and smoky and vibrates frighteningly, sometimes even shooting out flames. We do not know what it is for. Neither does Kester. But he keeps thinking of possible applications, most of them highly improbable and quite possibly illegal. This current enthusiasm, we discovered, resulted because Kester suddenly thought he might be able to employ the Diabolical Machine against the alpacas, and he rushed off to fetch it out. Not that he's a cruel or unfeeling boy, but when you see an opportunity ……

There followed a brief, but lively, discussion as Reeb and I explained, carefully and slowly what "overkill" meant, both literally and metaphorically, and how wheeling out the DM just to keep an alpaca at bay was not really an option and that we were not prepared to see a beloved pet sailing away through the air if it attempted another assault. Mind you, I have to admit that after another small skirmish with Monty involving a particularly well aimed gob that slithered greenly down my cheek as my hands were otherwise engaged and therefore unable to mop it off, my own opinions on the subject did undergo a slight change.

Eventually the job was done. The halters were removed, we stepped back and the two alpacas raced away across the paddock gobbing jubilantly at each other. Kester stumped off to re-cover the DM and wheel it back into the barn. And I limped indoors to have a shower and put arnica on my bruises.

Jay telephoned this evening for a chat. She's been busy helping out behind the bar at the Black Horse where her husband Darren is manager. Last night, just before closing time, she was talking to a regular who cycles over from Shefford and noticing, as a good bar maid would, that his glass was empty, offered him another drink.

"Better not," he replied, "I've had two already and there's a lot of filth on the road tonight."

"Oh," commented Jay innocently, polishing a glass, "I didn't think the police bothered to pull over cyclists and breathalyse them."

There was a pause.

"I meant," said the man carefully, "that there's a lot of mud on the road, so I'll have to be wary how I go."

Sometimes feel quite ashamed of my child.

Jay also told me that she'd seen a notice on the dentist's noticeboard advertising rescue battery hens for sale, and she passed on a number for me to call. I was grateful for the number, but I couldn't help wondering what the connection was between ex-battery hens and dentists.

Another of life's little mysteries.

And life's little mysteries also seemed to have exercised Ann's brain today. Her latest e-mail was as follows:

"A general and all encompassing Wot Ho!" (*since I was still a little fragile after my encounter with the alpacas earlier I was rather glad not to have my feelings assaulted by Ann's usual form of greeting. A general and all encompassing Wot Ho sounded very good to me*)

"Still trying to find some sort of hobby or pastime that Lam and I can share. Lam thought it might be quite fun to have a go at flying model airplanes. I thought it might be fun too, so we bought a couple from a shop in Plymouth and went up to Caradon Hill.

My maiden flight lasted an entire two minutes before the plane did a quite amazing loop the loop before nose diving into a tree where it splintered into a dozen fragments. Lam didn't know whether to laugh or cry (the spectacular disintegration of my plane in such a short space of time tickled his funny bone, but the loss of money hurt his wallet and brought a tear to his eye). Lam, on the other hand, found that he has a natural aptitude for this sort of thing, so, after collecting the debris of my plane and depositing it in the nearest bin, I fetched a deck chair out of the back of the car and settled myself down to watch him fly his big blue plane.

I have to say that I could quite take to this. He did a few take offs and landings, and, as his confidence grew, finally relaxed into the sheer pleasure of sending the plane round and round the field, swooping and diving (there were hardly any people about and sheep, so I'm told, make a nice soft landing!). I have to say that Lam is welcome to fly Big Bloo as a hobby, so long as I'm allowed to settle down in a comfy deck chair to watch, make encouraging or admiring noises, and take in the scenery. And if a nice soft blanket and glass of wine could be worked into the equation, so much the better.

As I was sitting there I let my mind slip into neutral" (*this immediately sounded warning bells to me. Ann should never be allowed to give free rein to her thoughts*) "You know the way in which thoughts drift around and float for some time before sinking into the brain and meeting up with a few kindred spirits?" (*I did, but I wasn't going to admit it*) "Well, two stray thoughts got together in my mind, had a few beers and chewed the bacon a bit before weaving their way in a drunken camaraderie around the old grey matter to pause sniggering in front of the door marked 'DANGER! Conscious Mind – Trespassers Will Be E-Mailed' and daring each other to open it, fortified themselves with a whiskey chaser and fell through.

Thought number one drifted in over the Atlantic, evidently following on from a recent perusal of a map and working out timing. It concerned time zones. Now time zones are fine in a small country (well, maybe. This is where the other thought butted in – and more of that later) where you only notice them when you board and exit a plane and re-set your watch for a holiday period. But what is it like to live in one of the larger countries which have several time zones? And, to be more precise, what happens if you move to a town which is slap bang *on* a time zone? What if it passes down the centre of the high street, what then? Do you need to wear two watches? One for the bank, grocers and butchers, and another for the chemist and shoe-repairs? You could get jet-lag just crossing the road!

And what if the road curves and the car park is slap bang on said line of longitude? You can bet your boots that there will only be one space left, the one where the time-line hits and you have to exit your car fast before it implodes under the sheer impossibility of being in two places at once or, in fact, in one place at two times!

And what if you arrive at work ten minutes before you

get up? Do you wonder who nicked your jammies? Do you ask (hopefully) if you are due for another breakfast? And what if you finish at five o'clock and arrive home at four thirty? Do you have to return to finish your day only to find that you are clocking overtime which, when you return home, you are no longer entitled to?

And how about when you are starting to get used to the idea, but you have having a 'bad hair day' and in your grogginess know that there is a time difference, but cannot remember *which way*? You could end up *two* hours out! And again you can bet your boots (if you have any left by this time) that if it is somewhere horrid (like a visit to the dentist or a dull party you did not really want to attend) you would be two hours *early*, and if it was somewhere important (like your own wedding) you would be two hours *late*!!

- And what if they have the equivalent of British Summer Time? You could at this point be led away weeping into a nice padded room where there are no clocks and gentle music soothes your fevered brain.

The other thought (cousins in both baseness and insanity) was to do with the passing of time *between* zones. This floated in as I remembered that I'd checked the BBC weather forecast for Bedford as opposed to Saltash over the last weekend and by chance happened to notice the sunrise times.

Now we are well aware that the sun does not look down upon our beautiful blue and green planet and say: 'Oh look, they have time zones for me to observe' and settle down in its hammock for fifty nine minutes before hauling itself out, limbering up and, taking a deep breath, leaping across the heavens to the next line before settling down with a G&T (as opposed to a GMT!) until its next constitutional leap. No, it floats serenely by, smiling down on the earth (except over Cornwall where it smiles down on the cloud wrack between it and the beautiful blue and green (very green) earth), passing smoothly by, oblivious to the carefully drawn and measured lines imposed on the map by bespectacled bureaucrats.

DO YOU KNOW WHAT THIS MEANS?! – It means that although the little British Isles have only one time zone – the *actual* time in any one given place will vary. Now you in sunny Bedfordshire, being close to the Greenwich line, will not notice very much because when the sun rises at, say, 7.00 over Greenwich it should only be 7.02 in Bedford. On the east coast it will be 6.55, so the blessed-by-heaven inhabitants of Lowestoft can snuggle under their duvets with a hee-hee-hee as they enjoy an illicit extra five minutes in bed. HOWEVER, on the west coast (WC – and don't think we haven't noticed the opprobrious nature of those initials!) and, not to put too fine a point on it, in SALTASH, we are dragged screaming from our pits SIXTEEN MINUTES EARLY!! – and in Penzance it is twenty-one minutes. That's twenty-six minutes from coast to coast!

It is a conspiracy!! We are joining the Cornish Separatists! We demand an extra time line down the length of the Tamar Valley! Legalise cream teas! Pasties in every school! Burn down That Bridge!

Hope you enjoy your lie-in.
Love Twall
Mowl

PS: I think the Cornish already know about their time lines being vandalised. I saw a Cornish clock in Polperro. It sported the legend 'Dreckley' (that's 'Directly' to you, as in 'I'll be with your directly') in the middle and the dial read: 1ish, 2ish, 3ish, etc. They know. They know that it is not really one o'clock, it is really sixteen minutes to! It has been carefully calculated.

Dreckley = now ÷ never + the square root of 'Not on your

Nelly' cubed x 'They foreigners coming down 'ere, over *that bridge*, axin' fer things and getting' all impatient like!'

The resentment runs deep and they are stealing everyone else's time to make up for it!

Be warned! Only come down here if you have plenty of time *to spend*!

Chow again

M"

I get the feeling that I should gain some sort of solace from all this information, but somehow I don't.

Chapter Seven

I got in contact with "Free At Last", the people who rescue battery hens, last week, and as luck would have it they were due another liberation run very soon. It seems that the women doing the liberating wait until they have enough people interested in acquiring such hens, then they arrange with the farmer to buy a hundred or so birds. We, the prospective owners, are instructed to wait for a phone call or text informing us of the day, time and place where we can then get the hens from the liberators.

It all sounds very exciting, and somehow a little illegal, although it isn't.

I duly received my call on Friday night telling me that the run was next day and that I should be in the car park outside the Kentucky Fried Chicken restaurant in Bedford (what wag thought that was an appropriate venue??) at ten o'clock in the morning and wait for a dark blue van. When I got to the car park there was no blue van to be seen, but there were quite a few cars with people sitting in them looking, I thought, a bit furtive. I looked at them, wondering if they were all here to collect chickens and, as the time went on and the blue van still did not arrive, I got out of my car and sauntered up to a lady in a silver Renault and tapped on her window.

"Er," I began, suddenly realising that my question was going to sound very strange if the answer was no. "Are you waiting for a hen?"

"You mean the rescue battery hens?" she responded. "Yes, I've put my name down for six of them."

At this a man leaning on a blue Audi turned and informed us that he too was waiting for the "Free At Last" people, as were a couple in a camper van, so we whiled away the time by chatting amongst ourselves. Which turned out to be not entirely a good thing. It seemed that I was the only one who was there for the first time. All the others were coming back for more birds (which did make me wonder fleetingly if they were all as they seemed. I mean, here we were with a source of nice, fresh hens selling for just £1 each ...... but as they talked, several of them very earnestly, about chicken rights and the cruelty of modern farming, I felt guilty for such base suspicions).

I have to say I was almost scared out of my wits by the stories the others were telling me about the state of some of these poor birds, and I began to regret having put my name down for three. Apparently they can look quite horrendous, featherless and beakless in some cases (the "kindly farmers" often de-beak birds to stop them pecking one another in their frustration and boredom). One woman said that one of her little darlings looked as though it was permanently blowing a kiss because of the way the hole in its face where the beak should have been located looked.

Well eventually the Rescuer turned up and we all crowded round her van with our cardboard boxes and pound coins. There was a flurry of money and merchandise changing hands, everything happening in such a rush with coins clinking, muted cluckings, feathers flying, car doors slamming and people rushing off that I couldn't help thinking that to an uninformed onlooker it must have seemed a bit like a drug run or something ...... a very strange drug run involving hens. The mind boggles.

Anyway, when the liberation woman opened the back of her van I was extremely relieved to see that this batch of chickens at least had their beaks. Not much in the way of feathering, some of them, but it was the beak situation that was concerning me the most. I was eventually assigned my three hens, and was very pleased with them.

Once home I opened the box and tried to coax Nicad, EverReady and Duracell out, but they were crouched down looking very scared and pathetic, so I had to tip the box to get them out. Somehow I think they were clinging on to the cardboard with their toenails because I practically had to turn it upside down before they finally slithered out in a heap onto the lawn.

Then they stayed there, just blinking in the light, heads turning this way and that. I thought perhaps I should leave them alone for a while to get used to things, and went into the house and stood at the kitchen window looking at them. Now these poor birds have been caged indoors all their lives, have never seen or touched grass, nor had space around them – and didn't know what wind was, or how to deal with it. And Friday was a rather blustery day. I watched in dismay as my poor little battery birds, not knowing that they were supposed to turn to face the wind to keep their balance, were bowled across the garden in a flurry of feathers to end up caught against the side of the compost heap, spreadeagled and cawing pathetically! Rushed out to rescue them and then placed them into a little pen until their agoraphobia subsided.

Actually, as the day wore on I was surprised and delighted to see how instinct kicked in. They began to scratch about in the dirt, they preened themselves and they flapped their wings. By late afternoon they even squeezed their way out of the trellis I had used to make the pen and crept along the hedge a ways before squeezing back into the pen!

So we left them out there all day, then, come night time I expected to find them huddled in a corner, easy to pick up and place into the safety of the hen house in order to be introduced to Attila. Ha! – no such luck! As dusk fell two of the wretched little things had left the pen to huddle together in what they considered to be the better safety of the hedge.

The hawthorn hedge. The hawthorn hedge strung with brambles and lined with nettles.

I looked at them and they looked at me. I called them hopefully, throwing down a little corn to tempt them. They would not be tempted. I tried to reach for them, but they withdrew further into the hedge, managing somehow to get through the wire mesh fence strung along the bottom of the hedge, so I had to go round into the field next door to try and reach them that way. This meant clambering down into the overgrown and muddy ditch (in my nightie, but with wellies on – not a pretty sight), leaning into the hedge screaming as brambles raked at my back, hands and face and nettles reached up under my nightie. I "chook-chooked" encouragingly between shrieks and uttered a few choice cuss words, "Flaming fox fodder" and "Stupid no-brained chicken McNuggets in waiting" being the more repeatable. Finally I managed to grab the wretched creatures and then, a hen tucked under each arm, I had to fight my way through the sucking mud and bindweed, back up the slippery ditch side, and limp back into the garden to the hen house before going indoors to pick out the thorns and dab TCP on my various wounds.

And if we don't get any eggs after all this ………

Kester asked me to post off a CD he had made for his uncle Chris. Apparently it shows his latest exploits with the Diabolical Machine. I made the mistake of reading the "Chriss (sic) read me first" file. I am still trembling. After reading of the "mistake" he made with the wiring, his improvisations, particularly the one involving a plastic drinks bottle, a hose and a pint of jet fuel, and his "near death experiences" (!!) it took a half hour lying down in a darkened room with something fortifying at my elbow to get my mental state down from that of near hysteria to a mere tremble. It is not good to have an active imagination and dwell upon the awful "might have beens". After resolutely (but with great difficulty) pushing images of flambé-d boy from my mind I spent quite a lot of that time giving thanks for the fact that I only have one son ..... although it did occur to me that even that is sometimes one too many .....

I hope Chris can manage to play the CD – I tried at work, but couldn't (maybe it had an anti-mother device installed by Kester in order to spare my feelings. The written word was bad enough – the video footage probably worse!), although on second thoughts maybe I hope he can't. Chris seems to give Kester way too much encouragement regarding his little "experiments". There was some discussion, so I believe, of the possibility of the Diabolical Machine being turned into a gyrocopter. I happened to be passing the living room door and heard a little of the telephone conversation – to which Chris seemed to be having an inordinate amount of input for a Responsible Adult. Afterwards I did try to speak to Kester about such small matters as airworthiness and CAA regulations which cover things that heave themselves into the sky, but Kester has somehow discovered that CAA regulations only cover air space beyond one's own boundaries. Therefore, since our boundary (apparently) is the air up to the highest point of our house (Kester is busy negotiating having a radio mast attached to our chimney. I am ready with a saw), and of course the size of our plot.

I am not quite sure how Kester acquired this knowledge. I suspect his uncle Chris. I've asked Ann to Have Words with him, but I know it will do no good. I am considering changing our telephone number.

Kester has now added a padlock to the door of the part of the barn where the DM is housed. He says it is to deter burglars. I suspect it is also to keep me out. He obviously has a fear of sabotage. That boy is wiser than he looks.

Talking of work (was I?), Richard came sloping into my office and asked what day Good Friday fell on next year. ...... Is it me???

Received another e-mail from Rugg. Sigh. I seem to do a lot of sighing when I think about my father. Or at least, they tell me he is my father, but you know I'm beginning to doubt all this "we tell you nothing but the truth" malarkey.

Maybe the gooseberry bush theory is right after all. It is very odd the way I can't pass a fruit cage without getting all misty-eyed. That must tell you something, surely?

Anyway, back to Rugg. I went to my inbox and found five messages from him. Surprised, I opened the first one. In it he went to great lengths explaining that this was the second e-mail he had sent me as the first one had been erased with a careless swipe of an index finger just as he was completing it.

I then opened the second one which contained the little titbit of news he had wanted to send in the first place, had apparently erased, and then forgotten to mention in the new one as he was so caught up with explaining what had happened to the one I hadn't received.

I then opened the third one and found that it was the one that had been apparently erased.

In the fourth one Rugg told me that he had spotted a small spelling error in the first e-mail and so felt he ought to advise me of it.

The fifth one was Rugg saying he had sent me an e-mail, but he didn't know if I would receive it.

This is Rugging at it's best. I feel it should be made an Olympic sport – except that anyone who's any good at it would lose/destroy/use for a shopping list/wrongly address the entry form, or get lost on the way to the venue.

To Rugg: to rummage vaguely; to travel without any clear sense of direction or destination; to send obscure e-mails; to dither.

Yes, Rugging is definitely a verb.

And that got me thinking of other interesting verbs and definitions that are not out there, but ought to be.

Beadflaunt: one who wears too much jewellery

Fuddlemonger: one who sets out to deliberately bewilder

Quiptomaniac: one addicted to telling bad jokes

Laminate: to lay protective covering of plastic over furniture preparatory to a visit from Chris

To Lam: To burst into a room (esp. unexpectedly); to bounce; to surprise; to smear (hence the need for lamination); to offer unwanted advice to impressionable younger relatives; to cause chaos.

Flinchwarbler: a person who lets out a high pitched shriek when lamed (see "to lam")

Snotweasel: someone with a really bad cold who refuses to stay home but goes in to work and spreads the germs to co-workers (see also mumpweasel, measleweasel, Ebolaweasel, hepatitisBweasel, pukeweasel, squitweasel and pukesquitweasel)

I couldn't resist sharing my thoughts with Ann via e-mail. Of course she got into the spirit of things and offered a list of her own:

Alpaca: one who takes a large amount of luggage on a trip to the Andes

Andes: useful items protruding from cardigan sleevies.

Rasputin: one who threatens with a file during an argument over tools.

Pullover: traffic cop

Prunesquitter: health food fiend

Numbskull: one who can remember numbers

Lampoon: jokes made about Chris

Space invader: earwig

It's good to have someone who's on your wavelength. Or does it just encourage one to greater depths of stupidity? Oh well.

Chapter Eight

It is very strange to be knocking on the door of fifty and have to go through the trauma of once again introducing your intended husband to your father. Nic had never met Rugg, so as we have finally decided to "tie the knot", an official trip to Wales seemed like the thing to do, but I was surprised at just how nerve-wracking a prospect it was. Especially when the father in question is Rugg. Combine this with the fact that women usually choose partners very like their fathers (and although I thought I had dodged that particular bullet, I am now reluctantly realising that I didn't), I have a sinking feeling that I am probably doomed.

The thought of the meeting quite frankly scared me. I expected my father to feel awkward and to do a lot of throat clearing and general Rugging (moving bits of paper around on table tops, sloping in and out of rooms, staring distractedly into cupboards for no apparent reason, pained expressions and working jaws). I knew that Nic would be on his Best Behaviour and therefore embarrass me no end. I am convinced that Nic and Rugg are not going to understand one another, but that I am going to understand both of them far too well, and at some stage during the proceedings I shall probably need to find a darkened corner in which to lie down!

I did think of asking Ann to come along to offer moral support, but then I came to my senses and realised that she would no doubt agree. But it would not be for moral support, it would be to gloat. She would settle herself down in the most comfy seat in the house, unpack her flask and sandwiches and prepare to be entertained:

1. by Rugg rugging

2. by an uncomfortably slicked down Nic trying to make a Good Impression, and

3. me getting very pink and flustered trying to explain to Rugg and Nic what the other one meant!

But in the end I survived the weekend. I think. Nic, who usually goes for the ultra-casual approach to sartorial expression, was indeed slicked back for the occasion, just as I had feared, and was wearing his crispest jeans and shiniest cowboy boots. This constitutes "smart" to Nic, especially when combined with a jacket. He doesn't actually wear the jacket, but it's there, and apparently that's what counts.

We rolled up at the Ruggery at 1.00 (I had done all the driving since Nic was suffering from a bad knee, which in a way was quite handy as there was always the threat that I would kick said bad knee if he diverted into any kind of foolishness during the visit.

Rugg greeted us on the doorstep also looking very slicked back: nice pink shirt, matching tie tucked neatly into the waistband of his trousers which in turn was neatly tucked under his armpits (where does he buy such mega generously crotched trousers?? I'm convinced there is some Old Man clothes shop where you can buy comfy cardigans, generous slippers and off-the-shoulder trousers, but you have to be over a Certain Age, and probably know the right handshake and password, to get in).

There was much handshaking and polite exchanges about the journey and the weather and a general eyeing of one another up. Marie hopped about in the background like a little bird and whisked us into the living room saying that lunch was about to be served. I brightly said I'd help her in the kitchen and, without remorse or conscience, vacated the living room, leaving Rugg and Nic to it.

So what can I say about the visit? Well, they didn't kill one another. Which is a Good Thing. There weren't any uncomfortable silences ...... well, let me modify that: the silences did not occur during conversations but when Nic, relaxed by a good meal and a glass or two of wine rashly decided to regale Rugg with a few jokes they were greeted by a confused quietude while Rugg gave them very serious consideration, jaw working, and the tumble weed blew across the expanse of floor in front of us. Then, with a small confused cough, an unamused Rugg apparently decided that the best thing to do was ignore the joke and move on to another subject.

There were a few merry tales about my childhood from Rugg, which were trumped by a few merry tales about my work life from Nic, at which point I decided to go and admire Marie's latest cross stitch project. When I came down I found that Rugg had removed his tie and loosened his trouser belt, and I'm not sure whether this signalled relaxation or preparation for a spot of fisticuffs (the trouser belt loosening, however, I put down to a need to give his nipples a bit of a breather).

We stayed for four hours. Indoors. It was a glorious day and I kept going to stare longingly out of the patio doors (especially when the conversation became somewhat parallel, ie: Rugg talked about one thing and Nic, thinking he understood (but didn't) replied in a tangentially incorrect way), but the hint was not taken and we stayed most firmly indoors, perspiring gently.

Just as I was congratulating myself that everything had gone pretty OK and thought we were on the safe home stretch, standing up ready to leave, conversation winding down back to platitudes and pleasantries, Nic decided to embarrass me by formally asking Rugg's permission to marry me. I rather wished the floor would open up and swallow me as Nic waited for a reply. It did not come. After a very pregnant pause Rugg coughed and shuffled about and then spoke quite a lot, without actually giving an answer. Nobody thought to ask my opinion, which perhaps was just as well because at that moment I might well have replied with considerable gusto: "Not on your nelly!" and headed for the hills. Of which there are quite a lot in Wales.

When we finally left Nic remarked buoyantly that he thought it had all gone very well. Then he settled down in the passenger seat, a contented smile on his face, and kindly allowed me to make the four hour return trip home. My nerves were still a-jangle and by the time we got back home at 8.30 I felt somewhat exhausted.

Once that meeting was over, plans for the wedding went ahead full tilt. Nic and I just wanted a very low key wedding, We had the idea that we could just stroll into the registry office, say the "I do's" and meander down to the pub for a nice dinner with all our friends and family.

Jay, however, said we couldn't do that. I asked why not. Jay replied with an exasperated sigh and much rolling of eyes. She then tried very patiently to explain that a Wedding should be Something Special, a bit Lavish. I said it didn't have to be that way. There was more sighing and even more rolling of eyes, and a bit of hands being passed distractedly through hair. Jay tried to explain it all again, this time with diagrams. I just smiled serenely and doodled pink flowers on her schematic.

Finally, seeing that her mother was a dead loss on this front, Jay took it upon herself to Organise us – apparently so we won't let the side down.

For the month before the wedding she bustled about arranging flowers and food and place cards and bouquets and table settings. I was not allowed to do much. Apparently she didn't trust me. I found this a little hurtful, but since I knew she was right in her assessment of my abilities in this area, I let the comment go and let her get on with things.

However, I was entrusted with printing the menu. When I proudly showed her the finished article Jay took one look and said cryptically:

"See what I mean?"

No, I didn't know what she meant. Personally I was very pleased with the alpaca watermark I had managed to put as a background. It was Dylan looking a bit wild-eyed and munching on a mouthful of hay. Jay was scandalised and said that I couldn't send them out. I said "Too late" as they had been dropped into the afternoon post, and felt I had scored a point for the rebellious mother.

Undeterred by this small set back, Jay continued with her organisation of the Big Day. She even spotted a suit for Nic and insisted he buy it. Nic naively thought he was going to get away with wearing something smart and casual. Kester too thought he was going to get away with just borrowing a suit from Darren (a size too big, but what the heck). They did not reckon on Jay, my Wedding Planner! She was going to have them both heavily starched and squeezed into suits with shiny shoes and slicked back hair and scrubbed faces if it killed her. Or them. If it came to it, my money would be on them.

I, much to Jay's approval, had already bought a very nice dress. I even had matching shoes and handbag, but I would not buy a hat. Jay tried to persuade me otherwise, but I would not budge on the matter as I do not like hats and hats do not like me. It took a trip to a department store and the trying on of several dozen hats before she would accept that what I said was true, and she finally, with a sniff, let me be.

I'm glad I have her (qualified) approval at the moment, but, no doubt on the morning of the wedding I shall be cleaning out the hens and feeding alpacas before scrubbing up for the Big Event, and Jay will be rolling her eyes and sighing even more.

Ann (with whom I shall have to have Strong Words) suggested to Kester that the Diabolical Machine could play some part in our wedding. She did sound a note of warning about unexpected explosions possibly turning the whole affair into my funeral instead of my wedding, but such a sobering thought did not inhibit her from then remarking that if such a thing should occur she looked forward to seeing the DM, with me strapped to it, hurtling towards her with a comet's tail of sparks, my frock up around my ear holes flaunting my flannelette thermals (how does she *know*?) and my hat (she was unaware of my hatred for the things) receding into the distance with four little hens, complete with posies and "Just Married" signs tied to their rear ends, suddenly remembering how to fly.

There was also a suggestion of Reeb and Small as bridesmaids mounted on alpacas decked out in orange blossom and next-door's sweet peas.

She was sure it would be a Grand Sight.

I told her to keep her suggestions to herself.

Unfortunately, now she has put the thought in the Owlmaster's head there is the horrible possibility that I could well step out of the door on the Fateful Friday and be greeted by a proudly beaming Boy standing beside a ribbon bedecked Contraption eagerly expecting me to hoist up my skirts and climb aboard. He (and Reeb – I'm not sure how she managed to get involved. Surely my meek and smiling little Reeb didn't harbour any hope that the DM really would be used at my wedding, did she?) did manage to get the Thing started on Sunday with minimum loss of hair and just a thin layer of dermis, so I am expecting the worst.

There was also talk of a little trap which might be pulled by the alpacas. Reeb was very keen on this idea. I have to say that if there was a choice of only these two forms of transport, I too would have been keen. The alpacas, however, were not. There was much chewing of cud, a well placed kick or two as Reeb approached them with halters in hand, and quite a bit of galloping. Finally, tentatively picking green slimy spit out of her hair, Reeb stumped back to the house and conceded that the idea needed working on. We did think it might be a nice idea if we tried to deck them out with little posies and garlands woven into their halters just so that we could have some photographs taken beside the little darlings. But they ate them.

Reading Ann's e-mails afforded some escape from the stress of the preparations.

"Wot Ho to the Old Boot!

Did I ever call you a bumpkin? Mea culpa, I repent me in sackcloth and ashes. A bumpkin you are not. You (and I mean no disrespect, to me it seems the only right way to rest in rural bliss) are a Londoner gone to live in the country and doing all the country things in a neat, clean and sophisticated London way" (*Does this woman even know me?!*) "which is fine by me and probably to the alpacas too.

Why this rending of outer garments, you ask?

I have been observing the Genuine Article. Paul, an acquaintance of ours who regularly leaves the odd goose egg, unannounced, on our door step. I'm quite sure that I've mentioned him to you before.

Now Paul, bless his kind old heart, has not been too well lately and put his chip pan on the stove to warm up (you can see where this is going) while he got into the bath. He emerged to four foot flames! Having been assured that he did not need the hospital and that the damage to his cottage was not too great, we eventually visited him on Thursday.

Sigh. Where do I start?

Firstly, and most importantly, we had a good look at him and, whilst he had some nasty burns on wrist and brow, he was basically all right.

Next we took a look at his house.

Pherrit, you must visit him! It and he are pure joy!

If Cornwall were to raise it's old bones up and don flesh it would be Paul! I can't possibly give you it all verbatim, but perhaps a little of the essence (eau de manure, probably) will give you an idea.

Sigh again.

Some of his lino got burned, but he will not be replacing

it as it cost him a fortune when it was new, 'back along ......'
What looks like a flattened cat is now covering the patch. He
says it is a rug. We have our doubts. The battered old dresser
is covered with books, papers and stuff, eg five tape rulers.

Lam: 'Why do you need five measuring tapes?'

Paul: 'Well, I got several vehicles, ain't I?'

He was a landscape gardener, so I suppose he would need
one handy (everywhere) to 'do a quick measure, like'.

I now know why modern beamed ceiling do not look
authentic. The beams go all the way across the ceiling. They
do not stop half way.

Lam: 'Did you put it there expecting it to grow, Paul?'

As for the rest, well if you think of our garage (a mess)
and spread it over two acres of land you get the picture;
three halfpennies in the same purse.   We hadn't seen the
place in daylight before – he usually has a bonfire (to get rid
of old fencing, etcetera (especially the etcetera)) and, so as
not to waste a good fire, invites us along with some other
friends round for a barbeque with coloured lights hanging
in the trees, music, the lot – so Lam asked if we could look
round.

I just need to back-track here to an innocent enough
conversation when Paul, due to increasing fuel costs, global
warming and a lull in work was thinking of downsizing to
a Vauxhall Corsa. He asked what ours was like and told us
that he has seen one he intends to get. OK so far. So Lam
innocently asks how much they will get for his old car by
way of trade back.

'Oh I won't be gettin rid of him,' Paul replies, shaking his
head. 'Well, I need the second car, like."

'What about the other one and the Landrover you have
out back?'

Paul finally admitted to having two cars and two Landrovers
out the back, as well as the car he drives. One (his ex-wife's)
is 'perfect inside, only the ducks have got on top and covered
it, if you take my meaning.' One can easily expect an ex-
wife's car to be covered with manure, can't one?

So we had the Grand Tour. There were *thirteen* cars (not sure how many of them were Landrovers), three caravans, numerous trailers and two old baths – 'they're for water, like'. Like indeed!! The ducks (and geese) were loving it. The car was not the only thing that was covered! And if that 'inside was perfect', I'm an alpaca's aunt! These items did not include the car he is currently driving and the caravan he currently takes with him on holiday. Further into Cornwall. Where else?

The fowls were wonderful. He said as how the geese loved the apples and spun a few into the general area (several areas were cordoned off (or festooned) by means of wire fencing, mostly to keep out the rabbits, but not doing a good job) and called out:

'Goose, goose, goose!'

('Well, saves me naming 'em')

There followed the most almighty squawking and flapping and honking as seven geese came charging up at the sound of their master's voice and started beaking into the apples. The hens were locked away and were singing to themselves, you know, the bwaaark, buk, buk, buk (I, of course, speak fluent hen) that they do.

He tried to show us his raspberries, but 'they dratted rabbits has had 'em! There was growth there yesterday! I'll ...... mumble, mumble, mumble ......'

On a totally different subject, you may (or may not) recall that some time ago I told you about Lam having a little kick about with a ball on the beach and how his gammy knee seemed to hold up well under the strain, huh? Well, in a gleeful and light hearted aside his friend Greg said: 'So you'll have to come and join our five-a-side football now!' Lam had been invited before, but as just the sight of a ball brought said gammy knee up like a balloon, he had regretfully had to decline.

Well, some weeks having passed, and Lam having passed back into his customary torpor, he gets a call from Greg who said, amongst other things,

'So, when are you going to come to five-a-side, then? How about tonight?'

And encouraged by a smirking Mowl, Lam foolishly said yes.

Now you may be aware that five-a-side is much more fast and furious than ordinary football. You may also be aware that Lam is now *fifty!* (Oops, sorry, did that hit a sore spot?) In the last twenty-six odd years he has done no more than just kick a ball around, not played any serious football.

Mmmmmm.

'I told Greg that I would just join in a bit and go carefully, you know, take it slowly and gently.'

You may also be aware that this particular Lam is an 'all or nothing' character. The idea of him 'taking it slowly and gently' and just joining in 'a bit' does not happen. With Lam it is the full monty or he has wandered off through lack of interest.

Mmmmmm.

So, I had a nice peaceful hour or two by myself at home only vaguely wondering whether I should have gone down to the playing fields to drive back a balloon-kneed critter (such a trusting and supportive wife) when I heard the car pull up.

Long pause.

Car door open, pause, then close.

Long pause.

Slow footsteps.

Sound of front door opening, closing gently, and slow, dragging footsteps coming along the hallway to the living room.

'Have you damaged your knee?' I called.

Weak reply from hallway: 'No.'

Then - enter the beetroot!!

'I am so HOT!'

And there and then he stripped down to his socks. A good dyed-in-the-wool Englishman that Lam of mine. Never removes his socks except in direst circumstances.

He did well. His team lost 9/11 (must have been an explosive game) and he scored three of the goals! I think that is brill, all things (his knee, condition (or lack of) and age) considering. The others in the two teams have all played regularly for yonks, they are largely whole (and for some of them the word is *large*) and the poor old Fleece is about ten years older than the next oldest!!

Today he is not quite well. I left him in his dressing gown in a chair.

'So how do you feel this morning?'

'Old.'

Sympathy? Nah! Why change the habits of a lifetime?

'Maybe last night was a bad idea,' he murmured. 'Too adventurous.'

'No,' I said brightly. 'Keep going, you'll be fine!'

There, that took your mind off the wedding, didn't it?

Love twall

Mowl."

And it did, actually.

And I had also remembered the fact that Chris had attained his half century, in fact I had composed a poem to mark the occasion (to be sung to the tune of that famous Christmas carol, the First Noel):

The first Mo-el the kinsfolk did chime
To certain poor lambkins who had passed their prime –
"Don't take it to heart, you might have fewer teeth,
But there's no need to worry, you've still got your fleeth*.
That's something to celebrate, hoot over, cheer,
To toast in the fire, or better, with beer!
It may be more greyish than brownish or blond,
So let's all have a drink and duck Lam in the pond!"

* *Poetic licence.*

I don't remember if he or Ann were impressed by it. Probably not.

Chapter Nine

Jay, looking very flushed and proud, said the wedding was a success. If Jay says so, then it must be so. As far as I'm concerned, the fact that the Diabolical Machine did not put in an appearance, Nic turned up on time, scrubbed and suited, and nobody forgot their lines or the rings, it was indeed a success.

The night before the wedding, however, I have to say that I was a little nervous. Not about the ceremony, or with second thoughts or fears of Not Doing the Right Thing, but because Kester had made vague comments about dragging Nic out for a stag do, something which Nic had adamantly declared he did not want. Knowing my son there were a tense few hours on the eve of the Big Day when he could well have taken it into his head to decide he was going to ignore all Nic's protestations and taken matters into his own hands. I greatly feared that should this happen there could have been a conspicuous Groom shaped gap in the wedding, and a very wide-eyed and innocent looking Boy trying to remain stony faced while Jay and I got him in a corner and bombarded him with vociferous questioning aided by the application of thumb screws. Nic, meanwhile, would have been regaining consciousness only to find himself stripped naked and handcuffed to a sleeping tramp in the baggage carriage of a slow train bound for the Outer Hebrides.

This is why I kept said Boy firmly under my gaze on

the eve of the wedding, and no such mishap occurred, and everything went swimmingly.

Well, actually there was one small incident. Or should I say, there was one Small incident. It was at the reception when Small was presented with a choice of two very sticky, very chocolaty options for dessert, and in a moment of excitement chose both, along with a large glass of lemonade with which to wash them down.

They went down very well.

And came up again a short time later. Reeb kindly took her away, looking very green about the gills, and within an hour or so she had recovered sufficiently to face the ride home and to feed her bridesmaid's bouquet to the alpacas.

Rugg did not give a speech. Apparently he wanted to, in fact had one all prepared and written out, but, since it was an informal affair, didn't find the opportunity. I should have noticed that there was a lot of shuffling of paper under the table, and a considerable amount of throat clearing, which generally means he has something to say, but doesn't know if he should say it, but I suppose I was a little too taken up with other things and didn't. I should feel relieved that he didn't manage to make his speech, but oddly enough I feel a little sad.

There were a few photographs. But not many. The trouble is that Nic does not photograph well. He has one of those faces where his eyes become bulging and staring and the zygomatic muscles kind of lock up as soon as a camera is pointed in his direction. I was not really keen on having wedding pictures where the groom looked as though he would dearly like to make a break for freedom if it wasn't for the barrel of the shotgun that was nestling firmly in the small of his back.

There was no honeymoon. I am going to have to work on Nic about holidays. He does not see the need for them.

Received an e-mail from Ann almost as soon as she arrived back in Cornwall.

"Wot Ho to the New Look Boot!

So, you're hitched again are you? That means I shall have to fork out for anniversary cards again. And try, try, TRY to make sure that I not only put all the anniversaries in my diary, but also remember to *look* in my diary to see what I was supposed to be trying to remember! Sigh, who'd have a Mowl?

Some of it (and here comes the Big Excuse) is because I work in accounts. Now most people would think that this would make you good at remembering numbers and dates, but this is a Mowl we are talking about, so life is not that straightforward. What I am trying to make sound reasonable is the fact that we operate a few days (and at year end maybe a couple of *months*) behind everyone else, so my life is a constant cry of 'How can that be the date already?'

You've heard some lame excuses, haven't you?

Serious paragraph (in case you were looking for the implied (or overt) sarcasm (does irony sound more intellectual?)): That was a really good bash on Friday. Jay did you proud with her organising. The food was scrumptious and the whole evening just fine and dandy. You have a lovely family which Nic seems to have slipped into it without any problem. I'm sure you will all be very happy. Well done. It were great. A truly lovely day. End of serious paragraph.

I was torn between a) coming clean at the 'do' about the fun we were all having over your wedding present, and, b) chortling over an e-mail. I've opted for the latter.

Started off thinking about serious gifts. Toasters. Bed linen. Tea plates. Boring. Ran out of ideas. No list provided. Grump. Then it starts. This is my sister. I can be creative. When you start thinking 'sister' and 'Pherrit' and then put the two together the old grey matters starts to boil over and go 'outside the box'.

What comes to mind when you think the word 'Pherrit'?

Animals.

Strange animals.

The Book of Revelation.

Plymouth, however, is somewhat boring and I did not find too many seven-headed, ten-horned beasts. Not even on EBay. I flirted with the idea of a dog, but already knew that you had two, so I thought – kitten! I knew you already had one mew, but in a menagerie there is always room for another mew! Aha! Images of glittering and be-ribboned parcel planted beneath your snout, mewing frantically, and two grinning guests demanding 'Guess what?' floated temptingly around the old grey matter. It was soon replaced by images of a horror-movie scene with a claw ripping out of the package and disembowelling anyone brave/stupid enough to come within twenty yards of it, and two manic guests demanding 'Guess what?' in high pitched voices as they backed away fast, picking at their already reddening bandages.

Hmmm. Possibilities.

The only trouble was – getting it up there.

I did think of getting a kitten in Plymouth and driving up with it on the back seat, but the image of you unwrapping a parcel of be-ribboned and now poo-covered kitten after being confined in a box for such a long journey caused some measure of ambivalence. The problem was not you opening the parcel and the caked kitten leaping into your lap, but of what may have been deposited on our back seat in the interim. In my car too!!

Back to the drawing board.

And then I thought: Jay! (No, not that she would make a nice and unusual pet!). Maybe she could obtained it for us Up There and we just call in to wrap and bung! Ideal. Then Jay spoiled it all by saying that you would not appreciate another cat, not even a cute, big-eyed kitten, and the idea sagged. Then Reeb was consulted and she added her assurance that the last thing you wanted at the moment was another animal, especially one that was likely to rip up your curtains and carpets, so the idea was completely scotched.

Things began to look grim. The pressy might have to be a serious one!

I hopefully suggested a tarantula, but Jay was not keen, and I had nightmares of it escaping in the car on the way up, so we abandoned that idea too.

I gave some consideration to a wormery – just imagine unwrapping that! But was not convinced, and panic began to set in.

Then I thought 'hens', and things began to look brighter. I had seen an ad for some curious little creatures called silkie bantams, and I decided that they were very 'you'. Immediately I telephoned Jay to confer. She liked the idea. Things looked even brighter. I thought that I had got it sussed. I was just preparing to invest in a hen-carrying case and shuffle off to buy the little things, when I got a panic call from Jay informing me that you had just gone and bought yourself the very same type of silkie bantams for yourself!!!

Stuff her, I thought, and went out and spent some of the money I had intended for your gift on a rather fetching hair comb replete with a generous spray of white feathers to wear at the wedding, and which (I thought) looked rather like the silkie bantam I wanted to buy you. You may take it as a visual raspberry.

So, since imagination on the present front then failed us, you got a voucher and this e-mail. And us. Sounds like we've gone back to the Book of Revelation – an obscene utterance and a worm that does not die! Gift wrapped.

Enjoy!

Mowl."

The voucher was for Nic and me to take a trip to a theme park where I know there are particularly adventurous, and possibly dangerous, rides. Either my sister really doesn't know us, or this is some kind of subtle (or not so subtle) revenge.

I can't make up my mind which it is, and it's bothering me.

Chapter Ten

And so, after the wedding, back to the humdrum of life.

I thought it was about time I cleaned out Small's bedroom today. Cleaning out any of the children's rooms is a task I dread.

I have always given them free-reign in their own rooms, respecting their right to free expression within their own space, and only venturing in when it seems that the oxygen/child-smell ratio has shifted to dangerous levels away from the oxygen side, or when I notice rubbish spilling out into the hallway when they open their doors.

I particularly remember, indeed it is seared onto my consciousness, the time when I cleaned out Kester's room while he was still living in the house, the chalet (or Owlmastery) not having been built then.

I stood in the doorway, black plastic bin liner and duster in hand, peering into the dimly lit depths of the room and wondering, with sinking heart, where on earth I was going to start. There was "stuff" everywhere, on the floor, on the bed, on the windowsill, on the chest of drawers, the top of the wardrobe and the chair, with just a narrow track leading from bed to doorway. And the smell was making my eyes water. The first thing I did was to crunch my way over to the window, open the blinds and throw open the window to let sunlight and fresh air stream in. I swear I heard the dry rattling sound of things, unmentionable, rushing for cover.

I worked in that room for five hours solid. I threw away piles of bits of wood, twisted metal, old crisp packets and broken pencils, mutilated toys and broken chunks of Leggo. I dug innumerable pins and nails from out of the carpet and the wall, sorted notebooks and papers into orderly piles, boxed up and labelled useful toys, things I recognised as half finished projects, electrical chargers, plugs and wires. I retrieved things for which I had been looking for months, like scissors, my tweezers, my curling tongs (???) and a book about bee keeping (also ???), and things which the girls had pronounced missing, like Reeb's diary and Small's pencil case (presumably to get a pen in order to write the blackmail letter to Reeb after reading the diary).

I managed to put a few clothes away into drawers and the wardrobe, but most of them were carted down to the laundry. Two full washing machine loads!

In one dank and dark corner of the room I found something that had possibly once been a sock but which was in the process of mutating into something almost sentient. I'm sure I saw it writhe when the light hit it, and shrink back into the shadows. It may even have hissed. It was grey, splotched with green, and faintly furry. There were even bulges that could have been the start of limb formation.

I couldn't bring myself to touch it. I brought Arfer up hoping that he would make a dive for the thing and finish it off, but he just stood in the doorway with his tail between his legs and gave me a look that said:

"You want me to do *what*?"

So in the end I went down into the kitchen to fetch out some spray disinfectant and a pair of tongs with which to grab the thing, and then I deposited it along with the now contaminated tongs into the outside dustbin.

There were plates stashed away under the bed upon which was growing mould that Sir Alexander Fleming would have given his eye teeth to have got hold of. Mould growing on mould. Mould that had eaten its way into the sub-molecular structure of the plates and which was not going to be dislodged even with the most vigorous scrubbing. Mould that had the idea of mutating into an evolutionary rival to the sock and waging war upon it and its descendants before making a bid to take over the entire room, quite possibly subjugating Kester to do its will in the process, and then moving on to dominate the whole house, and possibly the world.

I feared for my own safety and destroyed the plates completely, comforting myself that Great Aunt Florence was dead and therefore could not be upset by the fact that her cherished dinner service would now be incomplete, but vowing to deduct the cost of said antique plates from the Boy's pocket money. What with one thing and another over the years, I reckoned he would be enslaved to me for about ninety-eight years with all that he owed.

From the back of the wardrobe, wrapped in a slightly moist pullover, I pulled out an old lunch box. I did not dare open it. I could see green through the white plastic sides, and the lid bulged ominously.

There were things in test tubes I refused to look closely at. There was an odd stain on the ceiling which I also thought best to ignore.

When I finally emerged from that room it looked immaculate and I was a shattered wreck. Kester, when he came home from school and saw the bin bags bulging out of the dustbin, went pale, cast me a malevolent look and charged upstairs. There was a cry of anguish and loss as he surveyed his gleaming room, and for months afterwards I was blamed for anything that he couldn't find, and for the fact that his entire life was now blighted because I had thrown out the experiment that, once it had been perfected, was going to earn him millions of pounds.

I'm not sure whether the experiment was in the test tubes, on the plates, or was the thing that had once been his sock. Probably not the sock. I don't think even Kester knew about the sock.

Fortunately Small's room was not as bad as Kester's had

been, but it was bad enough, and even there I found things no mother should find in her child's room.

It was a relief to relax for the evening and find that I had a message from Ann.

"Greetings O Hairy Toed Varmint!

We are putting our new kitchen in at last!

You remember how it all started, don't you? Many (many!) moons ago Lam was working at Magnet and Southern and he bought a really posh kitchen sink (complete with shower attachment (don't ask – I don't know either! (but I have a nasty feeling that spraying unsuspecting Mowls comes into it somewhere!))) at a ridiculously cheap price, which gave him the idea that we could revamp our kitchen. As this is something about which I have hinted ever since we moved in this house, I of course jubilated quietly to myself because since it was now *his* idea and not my suggestion (translation: nagging), it could well get done. Especially as at the end of the week he then came home with an oven, hob and extractor fan. I mean, having got that little lot it would be a waste if we didn't do the kitchen, wouldn't it?

I got quite excited and went onto the internet to look at granite work surfaces, but after seeing the prices of them I suddenly thought how nice the chipboard ones are from B&Q.

So the new items were stored in the garage while Lam looked into the cost of buying units to put them in.

Now most people (as you know) when they are on the look out for a new kitchen go down to the scrap yard and poke about in odd skips and go and talk to ole Tom Trecobley who says:

'Ah, you be wantin' a kitchen, do ye? We-e-ell I've a mind that I done got one o' those in me shed. I were workin' over the Tregrundles' place, doin' a bit o'grass like, ooh, back along '74 that would be, an' they was after tekkin one out. We-e-ell, he were not more than thirty year ol' so I up an' asks if I could tek 'im. We-e-ell they says, just you go an' tek 'im back wi' you young Tom, so 'ere 'e is in my shed along o' that ole engine what I got from over Pengelly's place. Go on now, you tek 'im 'ome wi' you. I knew 'e'd come in handy one day ......'

Oh sorry, I forgot, you live near Bedford, so delete those last two paragraphs and read instead:

Now most people (as you know), when they are on the lookout for a new kitchen, go down to John Lewis and order the latest model which is then delivered and fitted whilst they are away in Barbados for two weeks. And when they come home – hey presto! – they have a kitchen!

The Humms, on the other hand, measure up, troop down to their local kitchen showroom and have the chappie show them computer-generated pictures of their dream kitchen (complete with two happy faces reflected in the lattice windows). They then ooh and aah appreciatively, smiling skip out of the shop, go round the corner and gasp to each other: 'HOW MUCH??!!' and crawl back home for a reviving cup of tea (catching their panic stricken and fleeing flexible friend on the way as he (this is Cornwall, so the credit card must be a 'he') heads off down the A38 in search of a place to hide.

Next we checked out Trago Mills (well, you have to if you live down here, don't you), but in this instance they were found wanting.

Meanwhile our fund increased to a fabulous £1,250.04! Luxury! – Now we're cooking on gas! Or we will be.

Enter EBay glittering with bright cheerful letters and the promise of never-to-be-missed bargains and dreams of sitting down the pub, beer tankard in hand, and holding forth about the Harrods gold-plated kitchen you bought for a tenner!

Well the first never-to-be-missed was missed because it went for nearly as much as the new one, and the second never-to-be-missed was missed as they did not reply to e-mails requesting what the cabinets were made of (it may be cheap, but was it wood or was it wood *style?* – Ha! We weren't falling for that one! ...... Again.

Traipse around other stores to see what they got. Not what we want.

Enter Lam with drill and screwdriver to see how we can make the old one look more all-encompassing without looking naff.

It can't be done.

Following on from that we wondered if we could make use of the old carcasses and just invest in new doors. Scrooge Number One lay awake costing out various implications and leapt onto the computer in his socks (no, he does not keep a computer in his socks. Grow up), pound signs flickering in his eyes, and began wheedling the online salesman. Fat chance.

Doors (can you believe this?) cost more than buying the whole unit. There was a reason. The salesman launched into it. But it was not a good one. Lam, still in his socks, marched down to our kitchen and pointed dramatically at our existing kitchen units declaring:

'Just look at that carcass! It's fine! Would *you* replace it?'

Personally, in order to empty the piles of stuff that were accumulating in our garage, and get a new kitchen, quick – yes, I would replace the carcasses. But I wisely said nothing.

Well, last week, as he was struggling to climb over the pile in the garage to reach a tool kit to fix his model aeroplane, Big Bloo, and barked his shin on the extractor fan, Lam finally said he'd had enough, and the dratted kitchen had better either be installed or carted off to the tip, and since he wasn't prepared to waste all that money, we'd better get started with the installing immediately.

We. Not professionals. Us.

Great.

So we have a painted ceiling and new lights. Floor tiles. Base cabinets. Work surface cut and waiting for sink and hob holes and joining up. We have some cupboards on the wall. And some waiting to be put together. I love Leggo. Lam has hidden his drill from me.

There was trouble with the plumbing. It involved quite a few buckets and some mastic to sort it all out.

We have a sick Lam and a sick Mowl, which is why there are still jobs to do.

We have a radiator. Wallpaper. Paint. Blind waiting to go up. We have dust. We have mess. We have splash marks of central heating fluid at surprising distances from the radiators. We have kitchen in just about every room. We have frayed tempers (and velvet). We have dinners from the microwave, salad bowl, chip shop or from any kind friend who is prepared to take pity on us (amidst glee!). We have a washing machine (we could have gone for another month without the washing machine – at the end of the dirty-brog period it was found that the Lam still had one pair of clean underpants to go!)

Things are happening. Watch this space.

Meanwhile Paul (of goose egg and four foot flames fame) gave me some potash for my garden. We are in the middle of ripping out and re-installing a kitchen, by ourselves, but Paul thinks that our garden could do with a bit of attention. Priorities, you see.

'That's *real* potash there, sister,' (everyone is sister – I'm sure he can't remember a single name) he said as he handed over a plastic carrier bag, 'not that rubbish you get in the shops!'

I looked in the bag. It looked like something you return with after you've walked the dog. Had he given me the right bag? Husband, dear, would you just stick your hand in ......? But then, O joy of joys, I remembered that Paul does not have a dog. So I did not have to carry out a controlled explosion in the shed.

The potash, which looks like scrapings from the bottom of his fire to me, is duly on the raspberries. I have some leaves growing around the bottom of my raspberry canes, so I have not yet killed them.

I am at work as I write this. Alone. Flu has taken out two of the women, Helen has a dental appointment, and the others are in conference. So I sit here, on my lonesome, listening to nothing.

Gad but it's quiet! – Too demmed quiet!

But wait, what's that? Is it footsteps? No, it's drums, slow, low, insistent drums, bouncing around my skull and eating into my brain, making me want to chew my arm off with nerves. The natives are getting restless. Where's my trusty old blunderbuss and machete when I need them?

Is that the sound of a howler monkey overhead? – and I'm sure I see yellow eyes blinking at me from the undergrowth.

Got to go. Have to weave myself a small hut and a camouflage hat out of old ledgers before I light a fire by rubbing two laptops together. I'm sure I have a recipe for okapi snout wrapped in banana leaves and marinated in garlic butter somewhere around here ......

The drums, the drums!

Mowl"

I fear the idea of Great Uncle Horatius is getting to her. It was only a matter of time ......

Chapter Eleven

I so wish I could share Nic's love of flying. It really is a passion for him, and a terror for me. I've tried, I really have. I thought that maybe it was just a question of getting used to it. I still have this feeling that it's heights I'm afraid of rather than flying, so I wondered if I could arrange a sort of Inurement Programme for myself. I reasoned that the way to conquer this ridiculous fear is to go up and down several times, preferably on short flights at first so that I can get used to the sensations and pummel it into my thick brain that when you fly you are in the hands of physics, and so are quite safe. Barring certain human errors or problems that I would rather not dwell upon. They do impinge, like little smirking imps to whisper in my ear about engine failure and bird strikes and aerial collisions with gliders or microlights, etc, but I keep a mental cudgel to hand in order to beat them off, and I think positive, cheery thoughts and mentally sing cheerful songs like "Raindrops on kittens and string flavoured mittens" and suchlike, very loudly. The main thing is, it is not magic, it is physics, like I said, and therefore basically safe.

Unfortunately I can't say that the Programme is working as I had hoped. For instance, when Nic said cheerily: "It looks like a rather nice day, so I'm taking the Dornier up. Want to come with me?" my immediate gut response was "Not on your nelly, old chum! I've had my breakfast and I was rather hoping to keep it inside of me. And beside, I saw a pair of rusty pliers in the workshop with which I thought I might pull out my own fingernails by way of entertainment today, and weighing that up with going up on a windy day in a light aircraft …… hmmm, difficult decision!"

However, I managed to clamp my teeth shut on my cowardly tongue before it made these utterances, and found my head nodding dutifully and a rather frightening smile contorting my features. Nic (never, as I have previously observed, one to pick up on body language – and believe me, every fibre of my body, my bulging eyes, the clenched fists, the rigidity of my frame and the sweat that stood in sudden drops upon my brow was saying: "Please don't make me do this!") looked really chuffed, gave me an affectionate peck on the old beaded brow and bustled about fetching maps and headphones and things.

Deciding that misery always likes company, I told Emma-Lee she was coming with us. Then relented a little and said that she could bring a friend, so we took her little mate Hannah from the village along with us.

Of course the kids absolutely loved it, encouraging Nic to keep circling various areas whilst standing the Dornier on her wing tips so that they could take pictures of Hannah's house, the village, our house, their school, the brick works, an interesting patch of bog behind the industrial estate, etc, etc. It was as Small was asking if he could swoop down above the hedge so that they could take a close-up of the alpacas that Nic did glance at me, notice that my fingers were buried in the foam of the cushion I was sitting on and ask:

"Is all this making you feel ill?"

I went for nonchalance. I think I actually achieved a careless shrug of the shoulder and maybe even a tinkly little laugh – I certainly could not speak as my tongue was cleaving to the roof of a desert dry mouth – and shook my head. Nic's eyes narrowed.

"Yes it is," he said with uncharacteristic astuteness.

(What gave it away? – the way my blouse was glued to my body with sweat? The wild bulging of my eyes?)

"We'll go back now."

If I could have unclenched and released myself from the safety harness I would have kissed him and soaked him with tears of joy.

So we headed back to Shuttleworth and did a lovely touch-down, with only a minor swerve to avoid the mole hills that had appeared on the grass runway, and by the time we rolled back into the hangar I was able to speak and smile in a less frightening fashion, compliment Nic on a good flight (after all, it was really) and watch him glow with delight at having been able to share his love of flying with a soul mate. Poor, deluded man.

So I can't say that the Programme is going what you might call well, but I really think I deserve ten out of ten for perseverance. There is the Inurement Programme as outlined above, and I have even signed up for days out. Like when Nic decided to treat us to a day out at the seaside. Reeb had a prior engagement that Saturday and Kester, upon realising that there was the possibility that, with us all out of the way, he could spend an entire day working on his Diabolical Machine without any curious eyes upon him, voted to stay at home.

So it was that Small and her little friend Hannah and I bumped over the grass to the hangar at Shuttleworth where a beaming Nic was waiting for us beside the Dornier. The girls were full of excitement about going up again and, as my mouth once more dried and the smile on my face morphed into a caricature of fear with frozen features, wild eyes and rictus grin, I wished I could tap into that innocent enthusiasm and look forward to the impending flight with something other than acute dread.

The outward bound journey was (everybody tells me) a Good Flight. We shall not mention the bumpiness incurred by flying just below a bank of cumulo-nimbus, nor the bucking of the plane as the air currents from the sea fought playfully with the off-shore air currents which caused us to land with a thump, take off again, and them make a second, much better landing on the grass strip at Clacton.

It was the homeward journey that was more ...... interesting.

Yes, let's say "interesting".

After a very lovely day on the beach doing all the beachy things like sitting in deckchairs with knotted hankies on our heads, paddling in the surf, running away from crabs and seaweed, trying to eat chips with sandy fingers, sheltering from the sea breezes which always seem to take a detour across the Tundra before heading for England, and enjoying other people's discomfort as they fight with beach shelters, we packed up our stuff and returned to the plane. Fortified by a very bracing day at the seaside I felt that as I had survived the half hour flight out, I could sit tight and survive the trip home. So Nic strapped me into my harness, gave the thumbs up, and I very admirably (I thought) refrained from giving him some other sign, and off we went.

However, as we wobbled up into the air (it was still very breezy) my door suddenly sprang open. I alerted Nic with a very controlled –

"AAAARGH!! NIC!! – MY DOOR'S OPEN!!"

– and made a grab for the handle, exerting all my strength to hold it shut, convinced that it would fly open completely and I would be sucked out. I know, I know, I had a full body harness strapping me to my seat, but somehow logic didn't come into it at this moment. As I clung to the handle, my knuckles whitening, suspicions flooded my mind regarding cruel practical jokes, life assurance, etc, etc, which I had plenty of time to ponder as Nic did a slow – very slow – circuit, apparently to stop the wind tugging at the door as I held it, but which my paranoia put down to an erstwhile unrevealed cruel streak in my husband who wished to prolong my terror, and we surprised everyone with a quick return to Clacton.

Now had we taken time to get out of the plane, have a cup

of tea and a tranquilliser or three washed down with a sturdy brandy, I might have calmed down sufficiently to bear the return journey with some kind of, if not exactly equilibrium, then at least a lesser degree of terror. But I think Nic could see my ashen features and wildly staring eyes and thought: "Better get this woman up into the air before she curls up into the foetal position and refuses to go anywhere."

So the door was slammed shut, checked and double checked, the thumbs-up sign was given again, to which this time I responded with a very ambiguous gesture (I could hardly control myself by now, but I'm glad to say my ethics just managed to win through), and we were off again.

Now my nerves were jangling so much that every bump and roll of the Dornier sent flashes of fear through my brain, my throat was constricted, my mouth as arid as the Sahara, my stomach churning and my knees were like jelly. I sat very stoically with my eyes shut for most of the time trying desperately to pretend that I wasn't in an airplane at all, but in a car, a nice safe car, trundling home down leafy lanes and that the bumps and lurches I felt were from wheels on tarmac, not plane on – well – nothing! – Lots and lots of nothing between it and the very hard ground three thousand (three thousand!!) feet away. I tried to lose myself by listening to my iPod, but somehow songs like "Fly Like An Eagle" lost some of their beauty, in fact they taunted me!

And just to make things even more interesting, the one time I did glance out of the window it was just in time to see a pin break loose from some kind of flap on the right hand engine and fly away, leaving the flap to, well, flap on its handles. Again I alerted Nic (I was very good, I didn't grab his arm or pummel and scream at him as instinct told me to, no, I gave the merest of nudges and a head nod in the direction of the flapping flap), and Nic (with great sang froid, I thought) merely shrugged and continued to fly.

To be fair, I don't know what else he could do. He could hardly leave the plane to do a bit of wing walking to fix the problem, and that was certainly not an option for me. I did briefly consider sending one of the girls out, but reluctantly decided that there were probably laws about that sort of thing. So while Nic flew, I stared very hard at the flap and exerted all my mind and will-power to stopping whatever dreadful disaster could happen from happening, like an engine stopping or dropping off or something.

I hope Nic appreciated that.

Needless to say we arrived at Shuttleworth safe and sound, the girls had an absolutely wonderful day and Nic was satisfyingly lobster red and happy. I was a bit peeved that my hard-worked for tan was cancelled out by the white of fear, but at least we were home, no engine had dropped off and no person (ie: me) had been lost in transit, and that was the main thing.

After such a highly charged day it's always good to wind down and relax with a good drink and something inane and frivolous to take your mind off things. So I was delighted to see that there was another e-mail from Ann.

"A Merry Wot Ho to the Old Trout" (*I'm not sure if "trout" is any better than "boot", but it does not go unnoticed that in both cases my dear little sister insists on prefacing them with "old". It doesn't do my ego any good*)

"You will notice that I am trying out a new greeting since you mentioned that you didn't like being referred to as an Old Boot.

But why not? – That's what I don't understand.

Boots are fashionable, boots are useful. They march into places like Poland, France und den der Vorld! Boots keep you warm and dry. You can splash about in puddles in them, stomp through mud. They make good door jams (can you imagine trying to boil down a door with a pound of sugar and letting it set before putting a nice little circle of gingham cloth on the top?).

You can hurl them at herons raiding your pond, alpacas eating your garden flowers, or daughters making off with your new shoes. You can even hurl them at sons before they manage to light the blue touch paper of the Diabolical Machine and blow you all to kingdom come. They make a nice chew for half rottweilers or a spiffy little hat for an alpaca. You can plant geraniums in them, place them by your front door and be the envy of all your neighbours. Hens can lay eggs in them – and then you can put them on. Nice! Spiders can make a lovely cosy little home in them. You can use them for splatting Mowls ......

But you don't like being an Old Boot. So what do you want to be? I'm trying out Old Trout. Let me know what you think.

To continue:

Greetings from a wet and blasted Mowl (and you can take that both ways!)" (*oh, don't tempt me!*) "Don't make me jealous with all your talk of sunshine, trips to the beach and jolly picnics on the lawn surrounded by sun-warmed hens. I write to you from the damp south west.

We had rain.

And wind. Pardon us.

We did not fly, swim, paddle (except on the patio) or drag out the bikini (fur-lined and waterproof). We sat and rotted. I blew my nose. Lam grumped. Agatha Christie goes down nicely on a wet and windy Saturday afternoon. I quite fancied going for a walk in the rain, but by the time we got washed off our shopping trip it really started to come down and was blowing a hooly (I have never yet found out what exactly a hooly is, but it don't arf blow!), so I cancelled the walk and sludged behind my book.

I suspect we do not have a drought down here. If they want to issue a hose-pipe ban we just say 'Ha! To that! We don't need to use hose pipes!'

I have been watching anxiously to see if the contents of my newly planted barrel have floated off down the road yet.

I have another theory about clouds. They are Londoners. Only Londoners could be that thick and wet – no! – I don't mean that! – I'm an ex-Londoner myself after all! No, clouds are Londoners because they love the West Country. Every bank holiday they pack up their suitcases, gather up all their friends and relations, and head off down here.

Some of them stay. For a very long time.

Some of them have retired down here and laze about sending out for pizza (or a cream teas) and get fatter and fatter.

But, to more important things! I am going to be rich! Did you hear on Radio 2 on Thursday morning about the chappie who had stashed away a pair of string pants and put them on Ebay? Do not try to imagine such things! – I did and had to sit down quietly for an hour or two and fortify myself with several cups of strong, sweet tea. The pants cost about nine shillings and sold for oodles of dosh. So I thought that if a boring old pair of unused pants can fetch a fortune, how about a nice cosy pair of well-used ones? Already broken in, you see. With character. And long legs. And interesting marks.

So, after we've flogged your camera (did you realise you'd left it here on your last visit? – no? Oh well, finders keepers, as they say) what do you think of this for an advert:

!!!HOT OFF THE PRESS!!!

A not-to-be-missed, once in a lifetime chance of owning your own pair of genuine secondhand, full-length underpants!

Truly unique! The trendy grey/blue mottled colouring is where they visited the washing machine whilst still inside the jeans, and the interesting red stain is where a pen was sat upon.

NO ONE ELSE WILL HAVE A PAIR LIKE THEM!

We shall then have a picture of said long-johns modelled by Lam with the ankles effectively tucked into rumpled odd socks (one of them inside out). Hmmm, thinking about it, maybe this picture had better have a large red 'censored' stamp set at a jaunty angle across the middle.

Three pairs only – all with individual markings!!

Well, woja fink? Do you wish to be the first lucky customer? – I might give you a special discount?

Ever since I thought of the idea I have been indulging in knicker-waving ecstasy and dancing around the room singing 'We're in the money!' and signing up for the chance of directing a more daring alternative re-make of 'Free Willy' (fame AND fortune – how's that for a high?)

Poor Lam has been quivering under the duvet wailing for his pants as I photograph them from every angle, but (butt??) I say, why pine for your old pants when you will soon be able to afford stacks of new ones? True, they will not be so cosy and chatty as the old ones, but (butt??) you have to speculate to accumulate. However, I would advise you not to speculate too long on the sight of said pants if you wish to sleep at nights. Or enjoy your dinner.

I really think we have a winner with this idea. Just consider the possibilities.

Seeya swoon
Mowl

PS: Ding Dong Dell
Pussy's down the well
But now we've put some Izal down
So never mind the smell"

I can't help but admire my sister's entrepreneurial spirit, if not her taste in poetry (and I use the word "poetry" very loosely in this instance). But somehow I don't think she's onto a winner there. Although, stranger things have happened, especially on Ebay.

I must admit to being quite jealous and could kick myself for not having thought of this idea first. However, I see no reason why I should not jump aboard this particular band wagon and fish out some very suspect bras that I have lurking about in the nether regions of my drawers (?). Better still, one of Reeb's bras would go down a storm. Not only do they have the requisite stains of interest due to reckless washing (there may even be one that, if viewed in a heavily curtained room with a spotlight behind it, has the face of the prophet Elijah spookily imprinted upon one cup. The Turin Shroud has nothing on us!) but they are BIG. The stick thin Reeb is a comely 30F. Don't know where she gets them from. Certainly not me. Both Jay and I are built on far more sparing lines. Not that Jay and I are jealous of Reeb.

Well, not much.

Well, just a bit.

Anyway, like Ann with Chris's pants, I see great possibilities here and shall take some time to explore options.

I wonder if I could sell Nic's Dornier on Ebay and pretend it was stolen??

Chapter Twelve

Rain. So much rain. And this is supposed to be summer. I am suspicious. I have heard of this sort of thing before, so I have embarked on an ark building programme. I already have the two alpacas, although they are looking askance at me and trying to remind me (by use of sign language and spitting) that they are two males, but I don't care at this stage, so I'm on my way with the animal collection. I used to envy Ann being so near the sea, but it looks like the sea is coming to me! – or at least a large lake. We used to call it a garden, but it has decided it would like to be a water feature, so who am I to argue?

Arfer is busy rounding up stray cats. I told him we only needed two, and we already had Phoebe and that she'd voted for Caffrey from next door to come along, but he said he'd do it anyway, and he would also bring on a few postmen if I liked. Well, parts of them, anyway.

Sophie is in charge of the pheasants, but she keeps eating them.

Reeb is busy knitting snorkels for the hens, and they are already padding about trying to get used to the little ducks' feet bootees she has finished and fitted to them. I said the hens could go in the ark with us, but Reeb thought they might like their independence.

Talking of independence, the Owl is busy loosening his Shed of Power from its concrete pad so that the flood waters will be able to gently float him away, and he already has his money wrapped up in a five pound note liberally glued with honey. He has proclaimed loudly that his map does not show the exact location of the land where the bong tree grows, but I suggested he make do with the Isle of Wight as a possible destination (I believe it is marginally higher than Bedfordshire. Most places are) and he grumpily agreed. At least, I think it was agreement. Anyway, he is almost all set, although the guitar and the Pussycat are worrying me. The guitar mostly because I fear I will have to listen to the practise sessions ...... I believe guitar wood is particularly good for veneering ark windowsills ......

Phoebe, having cast her vote for Caffrey to join the crew, is holding aloof from the construction proceedings and is assiduously practising sleeping to make the forty days and nights pass quicker by means of forty winks. Her dedication to this onerous task is astounding.

So with all this building, knitting, collecting and debating we did not have much time for anything else over the weekend. A roaring fire (yes, in summer) and a jig-saw puzzle seemed like a good idea on Sunday afternoon, and that was the extent of the excitement. No doubt Ann and Chris will be heading for higher ground to escape the flood, so I hope they wave to us as we sail by ...... and point the Owl in the right direction if he looks lost.

A telephone call to Rugg informed me that he is in the market for a lap top computer. For Marie. OK. Shivers started to run down the old spine. He had also been chuntering on (in the way Ruggs do) about "Did you know that you can play DVDs on a computer?" Yes, I did. Long discussion on the likelihood of this being accomplished on any old PC or is anything special required? Also, can they be played on laptops. Hmmmmm. We had company at the time, so I had to cut the conversation short and promised to ring him again the next day.

How long have I known Rugg? I use the word "known" very loosely. I am not sure if Rugg actually knows Rugg. A suspicious series of connections were stealthily linked up in the dark dungeons of my mind labelled: Rugg. It should read "Beware – Rugg" I know, but I was in a naïve mood at the time.

Link 1: Marie wants a laptop. That alone started shudders which defied exploration. There was a Ruggish mention of her having got the idea from watching Small on the occasion of our last visit. Can't remember, and dread to think, what Small was up to.

Link 2: You can play DVDs on computers.

Link 3: You can play DVDs on laptops.

Link 4: Various observations of Rugg and Marie warring with TV remote controls, and Rugg's inability to commit to one programme at a time.

Link 5: Rugg's recent idea to buy a small TV upon which to watch films and his "sussed" look when someone (probably Reeb) asked if he would be watching it in the same room as the main TV.

Link 6: Ruggishness in general.

Link 7: Several decadesworth of Rugg awareness.

Hmmmmm. The old dungeon shuffled out a quick image of the living room at the Ruggery: one film on TV. Another on the PC. Another on the small TV. Another on the laptop. And Rugg Rugging around them all fiddling with wires, knobs, buttons, remotes, volume, brightness, volume, channels, volume, screen size, volume – and managing to stand in front of them all, thereby blocking the long-suffering Marie's sight of them, for as long as possible, huffing, puffing and offering tea, wine, brandy and less volume to anyone who happened to be there at the time.

Oh dear.

I did ask what Marie wanted the laptop for (as in, what programmes she would like to run so as to know what size to advise), and guess what? – Sounding extremely surprised by the question, Rugg did not know.

One wonders if Marie really wants one, or if Rugg only thinks she does.

Was glad to have my mind taken off the Rugg problem by an e-mail from Ann.

"Halloo to You!" (*The absence of an insulting greeting made me feel much better. At first. Then I felt suspicious*)

"Greetings from Gloomy Cornwall! It is warm, though, so that's something.

At the weekend some friends of ours called in and said that they were taking a stroll down to Forder for the village fete, and did we want to come along? Well, what would you do? This world-renowned event, rivalling (well, on the same day as) the Royal Cornwall Show, is not to be missed! Mind you, we have missed it in all the previous years due to not even hearing about it!!

So off we went.

We trundled down the leafy lane and arrived in rural Forder and the fete (easily found due to the size of the place!) and marched in to the strains of 'Colonel Bogey' played by the Saltash Brass Band – and how much more of a greeting do you need than that?! There had obviously been a fancy dress competition as we passed several little mermaids, fish and pirates bawling their way home (losers, perhaps? – or doesn't anybody lose any more?). As well as the usual ice cream, burgers, gardening plants, crepes and secondhand books, there were some delightfully innovative things on display such as a motorised lawn mower pulling a few small seats, trainstyle – and believe me, *everybody* got out of his way! There was a test to see how steady your hand is, with a loop over very twisty wire which informed everybody very loudly that you had *failed*! And splat the rat. We all had a go at this last pastime, and nobody got the rat. It consisted of a piece of drain pipe (possibly a sewer pipe) with a gap in the lower third (for small people and Lams). A grey furry bullet shaped thing with a tail was dropped down the top end and you have to "splat" it with a baseball bat as it passes through the gap. Fun and jubilation!

Almost everything entitled you to a free raffle ticket for

the chance to win such splendid things as a stuffed reindeer (probably recycled from the Christmas raffle!) and a hat to which you can attach a can of pop or beer and which then has a straw to enable you to drink, hands free.

Such larks.

On another subject, don't laugh (although I think it is more likely to be the mega-modern Jay who cracks up, old Fellow Dinosaur will just blink and say, 'And?') but I have just learned to text. It is not my fault. I am happy with my clay tablet and stylus (with the occasional e-mail thrown in (and out again!)). However, we have a new boss as work, a fresh from London jet-setter who has to keep in touch with our office. Her schedule is hectic and (welcome to the West Country) wherever she goes she is usually out of mobile phone range. This is no surprise. We are often out of range at the back of the house!

So she texts. Which means that I have to text.

I owned up to her that she was the first person I had ever texted. Her face was a picture! She was trying to look polite while wanting to laugh and wondering what museum I had escaped from! Seeing as she had enjoyed that one I owned up to the other bit about regularly topping up my pay-as-you-go phone; yes, folks, regular as clockwork. £10 every eighteen months. I know that this information is way too good for her to keep it to herself, so I expect to have a reputation around the office. Helen certainly had a Cheshire Cat look about her when I went into work the next day and looked as though she was about to sidle up to me. I avoided her eye and kept up a meaningless stream of babble to whoever else looked as if they were not 'in the know'. My ego is thus intact. Ignorance is bliss!

By the way, I have some pithy comments about predictive text. Do you really think a mere phone could actually predict what a Mowl might wish to convey? Or how it might wish to spell something? Just for fun I tried a couple on it and so we have sierrit (Pherrit), jam (Lam), con (Ann – Wot?? – Didn't think that would be a tough one!) and heretic

(Horatius. Interesting ......) and it just plain refuses to do Mowl. It does m-o-w-*bleep!* And bleep to it too!
 Chow for now
 Mowl

PS: Intended to visit Rugg over the bank holiday, but you will not be surprised to hear that he got the dates muddled. I know that I do not really need to explain this to you but I really did say we shall be visiting on the WEEKEND OF THE BANK HOLIDAY loudly down his trumpet, but he seemed to think (or probably didn't really think, this being the problem) that August Bank Holiday would fall in September. Sigh. Fortunately I was warned by the non-phonecall I got from Marie to discuss the domestic arrangements and phoned them on the Thursday evening to make sure they were expecting us TOMORROW.
 That got 'em!
 Note of panic in Marie's voice, muffled recriminations sent in Rugg's direction, sounds (off) of justification and general bewilderment. After listening to all this for a while I suggested we postpone our visit, and Marie agreed with relief.

PPS: Two snippets heard on the news:

  1. In case you heard any news items mentioning that 'as Ann is now over fifty and suffering from rheumatism, it is not fair to keep her working', they are referring to a performing circus elephant, not me!

  2. Power from recycled waste: A place *just outside Bedford* is the site of this incentive to produce power from well rotted down, composted kitchen waste.

So I was wondering, hmmmm, a nice little outhouse, some well rotted manure (possibly hen or alpaca), and you could generate your own electricity. All you need (so I hear) to start a nice little compost heap is an old carcass. Any old carcass. A dog, possibly a sleeping demi-rottweiler, will do. Add plenty of scraps (following the onslaughts of the hoards circling your kitchen on Sunday lunch time) or possibly garden waste (alpaca chewed and spat flowers will do nicely) – and Robert's your father's brother! ...... Why do we say that? *Do* we have an Uncle Bob? Or has this been the problem that dogs and blights our humble lives? – no Uncle Bob! Would a Great Uncle Horatius do? Although somehow 'and Horatius is your uncle' doesn't sound quite right, does it?

Mind you, I have a strong feeling that Ol' Stinky would be a decided asset to the compost heap. We might even be able to spare the demi-rot!

If you go with this suggestion there will be power and to spare for the Work of the Devil (the Diabolical Machine) in the Owl's barn! Imagine that – the Owl hurtling twice around the globe on a kilo of alpaca dung and a carrot top!

Green is us!

Byeeee
Mowl"

Tempting, but I think not.

Chapter Thirteen

What a glory-be weekend it was, weatherwise! Very unlike Britain to be bathed in sunshine for quite so many days during the school holidays. It was so gorgeous that we decided to skive off down to the coast for the day, "we" being Jay, Reeb, Small and me. Nic had to work, Kester had just acquired a new (secret) part for the DM which apparently needed to be "modified" (I questioned no further) and I discussed it with the hens but they said they'd rather not. They were still sulking about the barbeque we had last weekend for a number of friends when a vast flock of their distant brethren were offered up on the fires of gluttony. The alpacas were willing, but I had no time to fit the roof rack, and Arfer had to be physically removed from the boot whence he had taken up residence as soon as he saw the picnic basket being dusted off. Removing an eight and a half stone demi-rottweiler when he's got his toenails dug into the upholstery is quite a difficult matter involving cajolery, meaty temptations, stern shoutings and (in final exasperation) crowbars.

There is always a little thrill about packing up for a day out at the beach. It takes me back to childhood holidays, you know, loading up the car with all the "just in case" stuff – swimming gear, just in case it's hot enough to swim, jumpers, just in case it's a bit nippy, tee-shirts, just in case it's pleasantly warm, sou'westers, just in case of summer storms, thermal underwear, just in case of blizzards, etc, etc.

A week's luggage could easily fill the boot, a roof rack and the back seats of the car, leaving us kids squashed into the remaining gap along with our toys and colouring books (just in case we got bored on the journey).

And it was rare that you got an entire week of the same weather. Or even a day of the same weather, come to that. Those were the days of the tyrannical B & B landlady, as I recall. Breakfast was at 8.00 sharp, and you had to be out of your room by 9.00 or 9.30 at the latest, and there was no returning until the evening time under any circumstances. If you forgot something, it had to stay forgotten. That was it. No exceptions. What? – you went out without your coat because it looked fine, and now a monsoon has swept across from Asia bringing floods and freezing winds? Too bad. Sit it out in a bus shelter, or buy another coat, cos you ain't going back to the Room.

So, we'd hike down to the beach armed with picnic and wind-break, stake our claim on the sands (going early, staying late to make sure we got our money's worth from the hire of the deck chairs) and strip off to enjoy the sun's rays. Before long clouds would usually muscle up across the horizon, the wind would turn to come from the north, and we were soon lying there using towels as blankets. I remember Mum (from beneath her heap of towels and cardigans) telling me in bracing tones that the wind was very tanning. I now recognise this as a Ploy. It was a way of stopping me whinging and wanting to leave the beach (and the paid for deck chairs – basilisk glare in the direction of that robber the deck chair attendant) in order to do something that might cost money. So I put up with the icy little breeze in the belief that despite the lack of sun I would still turn a healthy looking brown. Never mind the chattering teeth, the blue lips and the goosepimples that turned my arms into a relief map of the Pyrenees, I was tanning. And the sea air was good for me.

The only thing that could drive us off the beach early was rain. Then we'd trail off to the noise and glitter of the penny arcades and, as kids, scavenge around the machines looking for coins that had dropped into the trays so that we could have a go on the shove-coin or horse racing machines.

Anyway, we were finally packed up, Jay actually arrived on time, still half asleep, hair looking rather wild and unfed (Jay being unfed, not her hair ......), but still, on time! – and off we went. Considering the beautiful weather and the fact that it was a Sunday, the traffic was not at all bad. We motored along at a very reasonable pace ...... for about fifty miles. Then something happened to my car, Fifi. There was no loud bang, or plumes of smoke or even steam, but she just sort of sagged. I had no power under my right foot. We kept going, but now at a very sedate pace. If I had to slow down, as for roundabouts, etc, then getting back up to any kind of speed was a very leisurely affair, and then when we got to 50mph, Fifi decided that that was quite fast enough, thank you very much, and we stuck there. I tried dumping a gear, but it made no difference either to the revs or the speed.

We thought (after a very ignorant engineering discussion along the lines of –

"Are you sure you haven't pressed some kind of button, Mum?"

"You did put diesel in, not petrol, when you filled up?"

"What about that thing beside the wotjermacallit – shouldn't that be cleaned out or something?"

"It feels like some sort of governor has been activated. Have you activated a governor, Mum?"

"Well at least I can't smell burning."

Etcetera, etcetera)

- that maybe things would right themselves after a break. Perhaps the poor old dear was feeling a bit hot and just needed a cool down, but when we came to go home at five o'clock, the problem persisted. After the initial frustration I settled into a kind of shoulder shrugging acceptance, and we trundled home as if in a bygone era. It was very relaxing. We had time to admire the scenery as it slid gently by. I could chat and enjoy the music without having to give my entire concentration to the road and watch for speed cameras, etc. And for some reason – maybe it was the lovely weather, or maybe a curse had been put on the entire car population and they were in the same boat as me, drifting along with minimum power, I don't know – whatever it was, absolutely nobody harassed me, even when I crawled away from a roundabout at 0-60 in twenty-eight minutes, or stuck rigidly to 47mph (we were on a slight incline) on the main A10 with no chance to overtake me, people held back from trying to place their front wheels in my boot in an attempt to make me go faster.

It was all very spooky. And strangely enjoyable.

The time spent on Brancaster beach was lovely too. But brisk. And the tide was on the way out. So to add to the enjoyment we had a delightful one mile hike against a brisk north-easterly wind out to the water when we wanted to swim …… in forty-five centimetres of water – it would have been a two mile hike to get to anything deeper!

When Small and I wanted to swim, that is. Reeb and Jay could not be winkled out of the lea of the windbreak where they huddled drinking Thermos coffee and playing Scrabble. But as is the way of English seaside sojourns, they didn't realise how hot the sun was above the breeze, and got sunburned. Ha! We also had a merry time burying one another in the sand, but Small managed to get out before we had got out of eyesight, so the girls' plan to ditch the kid came to nought.

Yes, it was a lovely day. We even managed to have our traditional Sunday roast when we got home. I phoned ahead to tell Kester to switch on the oven where the lamb was already prepared and waiting (I never could get the hang of the timer on my cooker), and so, even though I had to do the potatoes, Yorkshire puddings and prepared the vegetables, Kester was convinced that he had cooked the Sunday dinner. Dear child.

Jay, evidently taking pity on me for having done all that

driving and now slaving away in the kitchen, kindly offered to make the dessert. I was surprised by this thoughtful offer. Usually Jay is content to sit in the living room sipping something fortifying as I do the cooking. I have to admit that she is kind enough to give me a running commentary on whatever film she is watching, just to entertain me, which (as you can imagine) is much appreciated. In all fairness I have to say that she does carve the meat when it is done, and most of it does reach the plates. So it was nice of her to actually cook something this Sunday.

It was like watching a prima donna at work. We had to clear the surfaces of all my stuff, Small was commandeered to hand her utensils, nurse to surgeon style, and do things like grease the pan and wash up afterwards. Then, in a flurry of flour and borderline bad language, Jay set out her creation. As the result sat on the side preparatory to being put in the oven, I strolled in from the garden to inspect it. Jay, a little flushed, artistically daubed with flour and with her hair in disarray, said, with some pride, that it was going to be a jam roly poly.

I think it had other ideas. It was lumpy, white and shapeless, somewhat soggy, and oozed red stickiness from grisly gashes on its side. It looked as though something pallid and deformed had crawled from the depths of the pond and into the Pyrex to die.

Jay burst into tears when I shared this thought with her.

We cooked it anyway, just to show willing, and I have to say it tasted rather nice. A little chewy, but very nice. Especially with custard. Lots and lots of custard. Jay said she's not going to bother next week. So, business as usual then.

On Monday I trundled in to work in Fifi in order to ask Mike, who knows all there is to know about car mechanics and, in fact, any other engine related thing, what he thought might be wrong with her before I handed her over to the garage for repair. I always think it's wise to go prepared with some information about the problem you want fixed, just so you can engage in some kind of reasonable conversation with the mechanic about it, understand at least some of what he suggests to cure it, and, hopefully, not be ripped off.

Mike listened to what I said about the trip to Brancaster and went off to look Fifi over, but as he went he shook his head and said he had a Bad Feeling. If Mike has a Bad Feeling about your car, then this could well mean that you are up Poo Creek without a paddle or a bailing bucket, and sinking fast. His verdict was that he thought the problem was with something called an ECU. I did not show my iggerance when he said this, but nodded knowingly, secretly wondering what an Ex-Cuban Undertaker was doing sabotaging my engine. However, I heard Richard say that these electronic control units were a bummer nowadays, and felt suddenly enlightened, and not a little relieved (scraping ex-Cuban undertakers out of my air intake did not sound very appealing).

Sat disconsolately in the office after receiving this news and tried to get on with some paperwork. My gloom deepened as I peered at blurry-seeming correspondence and held indecipherable documents at arms length while I tutted to myself about how my eyesight was deteriorating and that having to shell out for an eye test and new spectacles was all I needed right now. It was only after a full ten minutes of such peering and tutting that I realised that the glasses I was squinting through were my sunglasses and not my reading specs! – and nobody had mentioned anything as they had come in and talked to me, and listened solicitously to my complaining.

What with all this I feel I need a holiday. A proper holiday. Not a day on the beach at Clacton or Brancaster. And I would like to go on that holiday in some kind of reliable vehicle. Not an ageing plane or car. I sat in my hot, stuffy office brooding on the fact that it was quite likely that I had many more hot, stuffy, carless – and no doubt impecunious – days ahead of me with no proper holiday in sight. Then, to add insult to injury, rub salt in the wound and generally dance a short but vigorous jig upon a grave, I get a jubilant message from Ann saying they have booked a "quicky" holiday and that she and Lam were about to jet off to Cyprus for a week.

I could just imagine her dusting off the old sombrero and practising the Birdy Song and Viva Espana (not sure why since they were off to Cyprus, but maybe if they played it on a balalaika and threw a few plates around they could get away with it) as she folded bikinis and boob tubes into a suitcase in preparation for a week of relaxation and (perhaps) a little debauchery.

Suddenly wondered if I could haul out the crowbar I used on Arfer yesterday, hitch-hike down the M4, etc, and break into a Certain House in Saltash somewhere between the dates 14th and 21st of August, raid their fridge, polish off the contents of their drinks cabinet and lie in the garden, naked except for a large purple hat and fuchsia pink socks (with toes) drinking something cooling festooned with lots of umbrellas and a pile of fruit in order to ruin their reputation with the neighbours whom, I'm sure, doan 'old with such displays of foreign, up-the-line rudeness ("Comin' down 'ere, displayin' theys flesh. Doan know what the world's coming to ......")

So, no e-mails from Ann for a week or so. However, two days after they had jetted off to Cyprus we did receive a parcel from them, all wrapped up in sparkly green paper. Very festive, we thought, very festive indeed. And then we thought: Why?

It was nowhere near any kind of festival. It was nobody's birthday. And yet the parcel did indeed look very invitingly merry.

OK, we thought, now holding the parcel at arms length, this has got to be a Trick. It is well documented that one should not trust Greeks bearing gifts, but there is another, lesser known admonition, to beware Humms sending what appear to be out-of-season gifts when all the world and his hen know that Humms do not send out-of-season gifts, and that we wouldn't want them even if they did. (Oh, all right then, we'd be gracious ……)

It is also extremely suspicious that said gift should arrive two days after the Humms are safely out of the country and therefore unable to be questioned by the authorities.

Therefore, go the thought processes, the original niggling suspicion of Trick or Booby Trap is not so far fetched and is considered again, now being promoted to the position of Strong Probability. Follows slightly hysterical shout to the chalet for Kester to fetch long tongs and detonators, and to be quick about it.

See Small equipped with tea-tray strapped to her chest as a shield, big rubber gloves swamping her hands, goggles tied in place and long tongs at the ready being directed by Loving Mother with megaphone who has taken shelter behind the settee to pick up sparkly green parcel with tongs, being VERY CAREFUL not to jiggle it about or drop it, and then walk, VERY SLOWLY, out to the end of the garden. There Kester, resplendent in full Kendo battle armour, is standing beside the metal dustbin that we use as an incinerator, with the lid off. He then directs the carefully creeping Small (in a somewhat muffled voice because of the mask) to drop the package into the dustbin, and retreat immediately and at speed while he bangs the lid on the bin and dives for cover behind the straw bales.

A tense few minutes follow as we wait to see what happens.

Nothing.

Family go into a huddle to discuss Next Move. Loving Mother decides that we need to call in reinforcements, and as Small has now deduced that there might be some danger attached to this package moving business and steadfastly refuses to have anything more to do with it, and Reeb says we can't use her boyfriend Eoin, the alpacas are brought into play. They are lured over with the promise of carrots and the sparkly green package is gingerly removed from the bin and cunningly concealed in a trug of carrots and cabbage leaves.

Alpacas, unsurprisingly fooled by the cabbagelike sparkly greenness, nibble paper off package to reveal a box – and a card. The card is retrieved by means of the tongs and reads (cryptically we feel):

"Saw this and thought of you."

Really?

Thought of me?? Well, the box is long and thin, so was there perhaps something like a dead ferret inside the box? Was it some kind of warning, like the horse head on the pillow? The rest of the card read:

"Hope you like it as much as we did, Luvnkisses Lam and Mowl"

So, they've already tried whatever is in the package. Is it, therefore, half a cooked ferret?? Theories abound and a heated discussion takes place.

After a while we could stand it no more and instantly ordered Small to throw caution to the wind, wrest the package from Monty's jaws and tear open the box. Imagine our delight (and, it must be admitted, slight disappointment after all that speculation and excitement) to find that it was a box of biscuits decorated with Mucha's Four Seasons pictures! Once I have picked out the old bits of masticated cabbage and washed the alpaca slobber off it, it will look really nice on my windowsill.

Lovely. And so much better than a dead ferret.

Received an e-mail from Rugg today. He called me George and thanked me for a very nice evening, further informing me that Marie suggested I try bicarbonate of soda on the stain, and that he was sorry.

Chapter Fourteen

September is upon us and I suddenly realised that I had not bought Small's new school uniform which she needs as she is moving from Lower School to Middle School. Mad dash to Milton Keynes with a reluctant Small in tow to see what was left in the shops. Marvelled, yet again, at the fact that in all the rows and rows of clothing there is an abundance of every age size except age 9 in the particular style we like.

Managed to kit her out with the basics, all bought with generous length in arm and leg to allow for growth spurts throughout the year. Reassured Small as she gripped the waistband of her black trousers and stumbled over the hem that a belt would take care of the problem, and that, anyway, she'd soon grow into them. Also reassured her that judicious use of padding would ensure a snug fit to the shoes which felt a bit sloppy as she walked about the shop, and that come winter she'd be glad of the jumper sleeve covering her entire hand.

The first day of the new term dawned and I managed to winkle a sleepy Small out of her bed, got her breakfast as she washed and dressed, and then shooshed her out of the door in plenty of time for her to catch the school bus.

This is the first time she has to go by bus since the Lower School was just down the road in the village, so I went with her. She is supposed to wait outside Road Farm which is about two hundred yards away along an unpavemented road along which fast cars and lorries dash about at that time in the morning, so I thought I would see if I could persuade the bus driver to pick her up from outside our house. The bus driver was a very kind fellow and willingly agreed, especially since Small was the only one to be picked up from that stop.

Excellent.

So, next morning I positioned Small out by the gate and then went indoors to sort myself out ready for work. Luckily I happened to glance out of the window just as Small climbed aboard the little bus that collects the children for the private school. I charged outside and hoicked her off, apologising to the bus driver and telling Small that her bus was the big double-decker, and that on no account was she to get onto anything else. Again I went inside. Now I hovered near the window to make sure all was well down by the gate, so I was again in time to see Small about to step into the big double-decker – but this time it was the ordinary 142 that takes people to Bedford. Again I raced out, hauled Small off with muttered apologies and walked back to the house. I was surprised, and heart-warmed, to notice how smiling and kind that bus driver was, and how he lingered at the end of the drive instead of dashing off.

Eventually the Marston Vale bus drew up outside our gate and I went outside to wave my little one off. Again I noticed how very friendly the bus driver was and marvelled at the type of jovial people our local bus companies managed to recruit. He even watched and waved grinningly as I went indoors, evidently letting Small get a good last look at her mother before facing the rigours of big school.

It wasn't until some time later that I realised that my skirt was hooked into my knickers and that I had been flashing the drivers!

Mind you, flashing knickers nowadays is not the same as flashing knickers say ten – or maybe twenty (groan!) – years ago! My knickers are rather more substantial than of yore. A fetching garment cunningly fashioned from thick twill and industrial strength elastic, delicately garnished with Nottingham lace. They are shapeless, most definitely opaque, and rather warm. Some even have pockets. I have been banned from wearing thongs, firstly because of derisive snorts and shrieks of disbelieving laughter from offspring when I tentatively pick such items up in M&S, and secondly because there are horses hereabouts and I have been warned against frightening them. Even the alpacas had something to say on the matter. But it is unrepeatable.

Talking of the alpacas, I thought that the mating season was in spring. Either our two don't have a calendar or they are determined to make their own agenda because there is a lot of commotion going on out in the field at the moment, and the behaviour is definitely, according to my book "Everything You Always Wanted to Know About Alpacas But Were Afraid to Ask", some kind of foreplay, although it is greatly complicated by the fact that Monty and Dylan are both males. Indeed, it all gets quite startling out there.

Now I have to say that mating alpaca-style is not the prettiest, nor the most peaceful of occupations at the best of times, but when it involves two males who are not "that way inclined" it becomes quite horrendous. There is a great deal of galloping, crashing into fences, spitting and neck wrestling going on out in the field. They flare their nostrils, loosen their bottom lips and dribble green slime (it would appear that this is delightfully sexy to female alpacas) and then try to encourage one another to lie down (normal mating occurs with the female lying down with all her legs tucked under her. Don't ask) by charging at each other, attempting to trip the other one up, or looping their necks round the other one's neck, snakelike, in order to force their fellow alpaca to the ground. All this is accompanied by what can only be described as a very loud, high-pitched chirruping. This does not make for a peaceful night's sleep as a lot of this occurs under cover of darkness.

When the mood does sweep over them during the day I usually just try to ignore it. In the past I have gone out there with buckets of cold water and a stern admonition for them to behave themselves, but they always dodged the water, and the stern admonition was never heeded, and if I was very unlucky I would find myself on the receiving end of a lump of seductive green gob for my troubles.

If left to run its natural course Monty, who has now become the dominant male (although it is Dylan who usually does the woo-ing) will finally manage to give Dylan a good hard kick, then spit at him as he recoils, and this apparently means Monty has won. Dylan then retreats, allowing space for them both to calm down, and then neither speak of the incident again ...... until next time.

Unfortunately, though, all this untoward activity upsets the neighbours' children when they see it, and I've had to do a lot of creative explanation to their wide-eyed requests to know what is going on. On one occasion they called out to me, terrified by the thought that the alpacas might be killing one another. I went over to reassure them, and as I blithely opened my mouth to explain what was going on with vague tales of birds and bees, the cacophony behind me reached hysterical pitch with Dylan flooring Monty with a move that would definitely not be allowed by the Marquis of Queensbury. A lot of phlegm then began flying about, and I decided that if I continued with what I was going to say it could well put the little darlings off marriage forever. So I lamely said they were "playing", firmly turned my back on the delicately trembling children, and departed hastily for the house before I was assailed by any further questioning.

Rather felt in need of a cold shower after being exposed to alpacas rampant all afternoon. Also felt I needed to get my mind off the unwanted images that persisted, so was glad to find a couple of e-mails waiting for me.

The first one was from Marie, and I deeply fear that Rugg has now well and truly rubbed off on her (like something stuck to the sole of your boot). She proudly announced that she has done her first bit of internet shopping – and is wondering what she will receive ...... Words fail me. But the chortling does not.

There was also an e-mail from Ann, back from her holiday.

"Wot Ho to the Well Warmed Welly!
Wot I Dun On Mi Hols
I swum. I baked. I et. The End.
(This should be entered for the "Booker Prize". Woja fink?)" (*Personally I thought it more suitable for a Pullet Surprise, but there you go*)

"So, we arrived in Cyprus. And the smell hit us. It is always the same on getting off the aircraft in sunny climes, particularly a Greek island. That certain smell! No, not eau-de-donkey or essence of wild sock! Someone said it's wild thyme and heat. The heat is for sure, but I have not been able to trace that elusive scent. They managed to catch it in one of the biomes at the Eden Project, the one mimicking the Mediterranean area and California. One whiff and you are transported! – Your woolly hat sprouts and turns magically into a wide brimmed straw confection, your jeans shrink and widen into Bermuda shorts and your jumper flares out and flaps its wings, grows a few palm trees and seagulls to become a jazzy red Hawaiian number; your specs darken and the old wellies shrink with a popping sound to start life anew as a pair of flip flops. You are transmogrified (turned into a cat??) into a tourist! All that remains of the stolid wet Brit is his socks. Grey socks. Woollen and rucked down around his ankles. If there are no socks, it is not a Brit! You don't catch the average Brit without his socks on, holiday or no holiday. First thing that goes on and last thing that comes off (if, indeed, they ever do come off. Archaeologists dug up a five thousand year old Brit. They knew it was a Brit because it was wearing socks!). You can even buy neoprene socks for diving!

So we arrived. We hired the most disreputable heap of junk imaginable which the owners in a moment of enthusiasm during conversation referred to as a car. The only way we could be sure that it was not actually a donkey was that it did not have two long grey furry ears sticking up in front. Other than this it was lumpy enough, carried as much luggage, and had the same air conditioning capacity.

After the lush green of Cornwall it was quite a shock to be met by a moonscape of blasted bare limestone, dried riverbeds and metallic sky. We wanted hot, and we got our money's worth just in the drive from the airport to the hotel. We had to look up the hotel on Google Earth. It was in the middle of a housing estate and building site.

Just twenty minutes from checking in we were unpacked and in the swimming pool with steam coming off our shoulders and looks of sheer bliss on our faces. We stayed in the pool until seven o'clock, then went into the village to buy the statutory li-lo and illegal supplies (no food or drinks in the room, other than those purchased in the hotel – apply for mortgage here! – so half of our holiday was spent finding ingenious ways of smuggling in water and the odd snack). The first person we spoke to (a thoroughly miserable old bloke who moaned that he might as well be dead as working in here) turned out to come from Saltash!

Then dinner. The food was reasonable, but unidentifiable. We had to go outside and check that the donkey was still parked outside and had not ended up in the pot.

Then followed a couple of days of lazing around the pool. Well, modify that – as lazy as you can get around the pool. With a Lam. There was the usual ritual of getting onto a li-lo in the water when you are covered in suntan oil. A bar of soap comes to mind. The surrounding inmates put down their books and newspapers to watch. They nudge each other and move in for a closer view. They reach for their cameras and make movies. They laugh. They make encouraging suggestions. And just as you manage to heave yourself aboard and lie draped over the sides panting triumphantly (and exhaustedly), settle down with a nice book, some joker (who shall remain nameless but his initials (embroidered on his socks) are CH!) submerges silently at the far end of the pool and, like some terrible submarine, fetches up beneath you, jets out a stream of bubbles (!) and turfs you off your li-lo back into the water, book held aloft like Excalibur in the hand 'clothed in white samite, mystic, wonderful that caught him by the hilt and brandished him three times and drew him under in the mere'. Well, maybe.

Scuba diving was a treat. Welcome to the food chain, folks – you are no longer at the top! We were taken to a fish reserve to feed the fish, but the fish took one look and declined, muttering something about too tough and stringy, and so we were able to emerge with digit and limb intact. Some of them did try for a nibble, it felt like little kisses over your fingers. There was a bit of a swell on the boat, so we were both a bit seasick and rendered up that morning's fried donkey (I hope you are enjoying your dinner as you read this).

We visited some ancient ruins (or thought we had, but then realised we were looking in the mirror!). They were quite something, fabulous mosaics, bath house, amphitheatre, agora, bishop's palace and church. Lam kept taking photos of the drains. What does that tell you about a person? The ruins really were something, but it was *so hot*! Lasted as long as we could, then dripped our way to the shop for ice-cream (ye anciente ice-creame parloure).

Visited several other villages and did a fair amount of eating, swimming and messing about round the pool.

There was a very nice water park. Imagine that – they have a drought on the island, but the tourists can still have a water park! It felt very decadent, but it weren't half bad! Flowers, sunbeds, fountains, snack bars, *heat*! We went down slides and flumes, wave pools, lazy river and a glorified climbing frame whose sole purpose is to dump water on you. A large vat fills up at the top and then spills over onto all below with such force that some (I shall remain nameless) had to hold onto their drawers! There was also a dead nifty little ride whereby a person (Lam) shoots down a tube into a very large bowl, circles a couple of times and is deposited down a hole in the middle into a large pool of water. It looked for all the world like a very large toilet bowl wherein was flushed a little red-trunked poo! What does that say about Lam? – No, don't go there! Maybe that explains his affinity with drains!

A trip to the mountains was nice. Much cooler and greener and, therefore, refreshing. I found a nice walk through the woods alongside a stream, down to their famous (world famous in Cyprus!) Caledonia Falls (sounds like a drunken Scotsman to me!). Well, trickle. The only comments I can make about the descent are:

1. We needed a ladder

2. We were rendered rather wary knowing that this nice steep descent meant a gruelling steep *ascent.* And –

3. I was followed round by the smell of burning martyr as Lam mumbled and grumbled about the steepness, return journey, what *exactly* was I hoping to see down there? This *is* the falls, you know that, don't you? No, I'm all right, you wanted to come here, let's carry on, etc, etc, mumble, mumble, moan, burn.

We eventually arrived at the falls (trickle), took pictures and went back – Lam leading like Speedy Gonzales and leaving me toiling along behind as best I could. The next day he was telling everybody how much he enjoyed it. (?!)

We went to Nicosia. We saw the touristy bits and the ancient city walls with buttresses and gates. And more burning martyr. Left quite quickly without seeing much of it.

So all in all we had a wonderful time. We were like two pigs in clover. Warm clover. With a pool and a glass of chilled wine. What more could you want?

Luv twall

Mowl

PS: Got an e-mail today from Rugg thanking me for the card. I did not send Rugg a card. I did not send anybody a card. I asked him who had signed the bottom of the card and he said he couldn't read it and so had assumed it was from me. Apparently my writing is illegible, so any card he can't read must come from me. Even though it came from Spain and I was holidaying in Cyprus.

PPS: On the Saturday after we got home it was so lovely that we thought: 'Wa-hey! – An Indian summer, how lovely!' So off we went to the beach. Well, sadly summer really has gone. It is now autumn. Where did we go? – Was it Frinton or Frome? – Fuertaventura? – or F-f-f-freezing!!! – That's Freathy to you. I was all for going in, but it was Lam (would you believe?) who led the way, streaking down the beach towards the sea. Then had to go back for his trunks. And his socks. Well, the "streak" finished just short of the waves, after which it became a very slow creep, with many an ooh, ah and oh, that's *cold!* We dunked. We screamed. We exited. We sat on the beach with a book. And a shirt. We want medals. We deserve them. We shall NOT be here on New Year's Day!"

If Ann is going for the sympathy vote with that little PPS about freezing on a Cornish beach after gloating about a Cyprus holiday, she's got another think coming!

Chapter Fifteen

October came in golden and mellow. The starlings are gathering preparatory to setting off on their annual migration. They congregate on our roof, jostling one another and pushing each other down the chimney.

Starlings down the chimney is a regular occurrence at this time of year and Reeb has become quite adept at fielding the things as soon as they shoot, sooty and startled, into our hearth, and then releasing them back into the wild. The first thing we know of this invasion is a low thrumming sound and a small shower of soot as the doomed creature beats its wings inside the flue trying to get upwards. Which of course it can't.

Then you wait.

Sometimes it's just a few minutes before the thrumming becomes louder as the bird descends; sometimes it's about half an hour. Once it was all night! We think the little blighter roosted on the ledge where the chimney bends because night had fallen, and it slept there until morning when it finally emerged. All I can say is, thank goodness hens can't fly that high or they would be forever daring one another to balance on the chimney pot, and not succeeding; and a wedged hen would be a heck of a thing to have to dislodge from the chimney!

All this holiday bustle and excitement on the rooftops, and the fact that the October sun had such an appealing warmth to it, my thoughts turned to holidays, especially as we have not had a proper one this year, only a few days out. So when Ann and Chris said: "Hey, why don't you all come camping with us for a long weekend down in Devon during the school half term?" I foolishly thought: "Hey, why not?"

Of course *now* I know why not, but back then I was naïve and innocent. In future I will know to say, "Listen, Bud, if it ain't five star, I don't want to know".

Actually I have changed – and I could change again (a woman's prerogative, so I am told, and I intend to milk that for all it's worth). Years ago I used to be a very back-to-nature sort of person and loved basic camping. But just recently I feel the need for pampering during my leisure times. I suspect it is the fault of the hens – and the alpacas – and the dogs – and the bees – and (hey, let's not leave anyone out in this blame fest!) Nic and the children. After coming home from work it seems that all I do is housework, gardening or tending to animals, so there isn't much of what you'd call real sit-down-and-do-nothing leisure time in my life. No doubt my original gung-ho attitude will re-assert itself and I shall once again thrill to thoughts of mud, wind and outside sanitation. But not yet.

This year it was a simple choice: camping with Ann and Chris, or no holiday at all. I looked into the spaniel-like eyes of my kinder, and foolishly opted for the camping idea.

I must admit I was a little dubious about the whole venture from the start, especially when Jay said that she would like to join the expedition. Now don't get me wrong, I love having Jay around and I love going on holiday with her, especially now she's left home and not with us all the time. But she is very much the sophisticated young woman (don't know where she gets this sophistication; certainly not from me) and loves her creature comforts, and the thought of Jay under canvas was something that I had great difficulty imagining.

Another problem, which on the face of it does not seem

like a problem is that I am one of life's optimists. This should be a Good Quality. Not, however, when it comes to camping. I have now learned, through bitter experience, that it is best to be a pessimist when contemplating any amount of time camping in the Great Outdoors.

However, I allowed myself to be swept along with everyone else's enthusiasm and arranged a date with Ann. I mentioned the proposed trip to Nic, but he said that we had a rush job on at work and he could not be spared. Apparently I could, but he couldn't. I had my suspicions, but although I fixed him with a hard stare Nic returned my gaze with unblinking, wide-eyed innocence and I had to let the matter drop.

So it was that Ann and Chris drove up from Cornwall, we drove down from Bedfordshire, and we met in a field in Modbury where we pitched tent on a very pleasant site attached to a large caravan site.

Ann and Chris are the proud owners of an enormous, old-fashioned tent they affectionately call Monstro. It has a lot of poles. It took Chris and Kester two solid hours and some very borderline bad language to erect. It has three double bedrooms, a living area, kitchen area, a larder and curtains. It is a veritable home from home. It was suggested that we all sleep in Monstro, but I wanted to sleep alone for two reasons: a) I feel uncomfortable about sleeping in close proximity to other people (except Nic. I've got used to Nic. Apparently it's in the marriage vows that you have to share a bed, so what are you gonna do?), and b) the embarrassment caused by my mutinous bladder making demands on me during the dark hours, which it does. Often. So I had brought along the two dwarf dome tent Kester used to use for camp-outs in our back garden when he was younger. I must admit I had been under the elusion it was a two *man* tent, but I soon found out my mistake. Once the double mattress was inflated there wasn't much room inside, either length ways or heightwise. Still, it was only for me to sleep in, so I wasn't really worried.

Come night time, after a very satisfying dinner of burnt

sausages and beans (you know you're camping when you're presented with a plate of burnt sausages and lukewarm beans) I bade everyone a cheery goodnight and crawled into my hive. It was a few minutes later I discovered the above mentioned truism about optimism being no good to go camping with. At home I found the nights recently very warm, so I had not been much bothered by the fact that I had been unable to borrow a sleeping bag for myself for this trip. I had merely brought along three blankets, convinced that the weather would be fine.

Optimism, see. Big mistake.

The night was cold. In fact the night felt freezing. Funnily enough I was all right from above, but the heat seemed to be drained out of me from below, despite being on a big mattress, and I had never felt so cold in all my life. So I wrapped myself up in my blankets and tried a bit of positive thinking with images of roaring fires and hot sandy beaches, and actually managed to get to sleep.

About midnight I was woken by a noise. It could have been an owl. It could have been a neighbour returning late to their tent. It could have been a psychopath bent on a killing spree. Whatever it was, it had me wide awake and listening intently, suddenly wishing I had thought to arm myself with some kind of weapon, and wondering how on earth I had allowed myself to be talked into agreeing to spending the night out in the depths of the English countryside where wild animals and weirdoes of every description lurked and hunted.

It was as I lay nervously in the darkness, shivering and listening, that I realised that I was not just cold, but also wet. It was pouring with rain outside and because my head was jammed against one canvas wall, and my feet were sticking out of the doorway, I was getting soaked from both ends.

It was at this point that my bladder decided to make a contribution to the proceedings. It suggested, rather urgently, that if I didn't want my back teeth to start swimming I should go outside and relieve it of the gallon of liquid it insisted it was holding. I suggested, equally firmly, that I should stay where I was and wait for morning. My bladder became threatening and remarked diffidently that I might not like to get wet from yet another direction, would I? My arguments became weaker, and in the end I struggled out of my blankets, out of the tent and into the pouring rain. I could not face the hundred metre trek to the toilet block, so made do with a handy hedge into which I deposited about a teaspoonful of wee.

Returned to the tent, bladder smug, me wet.

Now I was *really* cold. And it was only 1.30a.m. Lay shivering damply listening to the drips hitting soggy blanket for the next three and a half hours, hugging my pillow to me and wondering how long it took a person to die of hypothermia, and wondering if the children would miss me when I was gone.

At five o'clock I could stand it no longer and I sneaked into Monstro, located the girls' sleeping compartment, fell amongst them and proceeded to suck the warmth out of those kids, unheeding of their vociferous protests.

The next night Chris refused to let me sleep in my hive but made Kester give up his bedroom so that Reeb, Small and I could sleep in there. Kester was slipped into the narrow space between Jay's room and Ann and Chris's which was designated the wardrobe. So all should have been well. Only this night, although dry, was colder than the last – much colder. And I discovered that Monstro was pitched on a slight slope. This meant that I kept waking up during the night to rescue all my blankets which migrated southwards along with a slippery little Emma-Lee. Apparently everyone except Jessica had quite an active time that night. Chris found that Kester's face was about three inches from his ear, separated by only a thin bit of cotton (the wall of the wardrobe), and that Kester snored unless dug firmly in the ribs at regular intervals.

Jay, clad in Chris's scuba-diving "woolly bear" combos, zipped snuggly in her own sleeping bag and alone in her compartment, slept very well, thank you very much, although she insisted the night had been hell.

The daylight hours of our camping trip were boring by comparison with the night times. I shall have to give it great consideration before I can decide whether we had a good time or not. All in all, I think we did.

I received a short e-mail from Ann the evening we got home from the camping holiday.

"Good evening Flea Bag!

Just thought we'd let you know we got home safe and sound and to let you know that you left your leather jacket on the back seat of our car after we went to the beach yesterday. Lam says 'Finders keepers', so this is really just a courtesy message to let you know where it is if you are looking for it. Lam also says that since you wrested your camera back from him before he managed to sell it, he is going to flog the jacket instead as it looks like a good one.

Byeeee! – Mowl"

Always ones for the main chance, my relatives. I wonder how much they're putting it on for. I'd quite like to buy it back.

Chapter Sixteen

It is the first day of November. I only mention it because the first of every month is a time of tension in our household due to the fact that the "pinch and a punch, it's the first of the month" game is played, and taken very seriously. I sneaked downstairs to make the tea at a quarter past seven, being everso quiet so as not to disturb anyone. My plan was to take a cup of tea upstairs to Reeb, bend lovingly over her and waken her with a motherly kiss – and then pinch and punch her whilst she was still drowsy, thus neatly spoiling her day.

However, I was just pouring the hot water into the tea pot when the kitchen door burst open and Reeb came roaring across the floor, claws outstretched, and pinched and punched me before I could relieve myself of the kettle and defend myself. Reeb then did a little jubilation dance (I've won most of this year) and we both went off to leap on an unsuspecting Small.

I don't know what it is about leaping out at one another, but Nic and I have got into the habit of it as well, even at work. There are quite a lot of doors between his office and mine, and very often one or other of us will hide behind one in order to scare the other. It is particularly good when one party has gone off to the toilet. The other week I heard Nic sloping off for a bladder break and I quickly finished off the typing I was doing, then nipped along to his office (checking all the doors along the way, because you never can tell with husbands) and then hid myself behind the door there. I was giggling to myself and peeping out through the gap between door and jamb when Nic leapt out at me from behind – he'd doubled back from the loo and hidden himself under his desk!

It did occur to me that perhaps this isn't really suitable behaviour for such elderly people, but what the heck.

As an aside, there was a time when it was thought that our family came from a long and venerable line of devout Roman Catholics. This is because quite a few of our ancestors' remains were found locked away in priest holes in castles and manor houses up and down England. I doubt this. My own explanation is that they were hiding in what they took for a very handy little cupboard, giggling to themselves, ready to leap out at some unsuspecting person in order to "pinch and punch" them, but the door clicked shut and they were unable to get out.

That's what I tell the children anyway. It makes for a colourful past, and teaches them not to lock themselves in cupboards. A double bonus, I rather think.

It is very sad to think that the highlight of one's day, not to say week or even month, is to win at such a juvenile game as "pinch and punch". Ann always manages to send me such interesting e-mails, and I feel really bad about not being able to entertain her as she does me. I've been giving this a lot of thought recently, and it occurred to me that if I didn't have any adventures of my own to report, then perhaps I could pass on the exploits of somebody else.

And who better than Great Uncle Horatius, an old reprobate kinsman who would sometimes pitch up at inconvenient times and make camp in our coal bunker singing camp fire songs, smoking bad cigars and boiling up jumbucks. Truth to tell, nobody has heard anything from him for a few years, but just the other day I got a much battered envelope that looked like it had travelled many miles in a dampened saddlebag, been dropped in unspeakable puddles and rubbed against something unidentifiable but evidently furry before dropping into the British postal system and then being handed over to me. Handed over rather than put through the letterbox because it had not been stamped and had therefore incurred a substantial amount of postal charges. As I handed over the twelve pounds sixty-eight pence I realised that it could only be a missive from the Old Reprobate himself, and I would have demanded my money back had the postman not been beating a hasty retreat down the drive, wiping his hands on his trouser legs.

After spraying the envelope with disinfectant, I cut it open and pulled out the letter, which read as follows:

"Wot Ho Seething Flea Bag!" (*Great Uncle H can be so hurtful at times. And I now see where Ann possibly gets her own jubilant disrespect from*)

"Thought it was about time I sent you greetings to let you know that I am still shuffling about on this mortal coil and have not fallen foul of the Grim Reaper as yet. Correspondence is difficult when you're sculling your way up the Limpopo River under cover of darkness with a herd of slavering crocs sniffing at your heels, and also, as I said to my old mate Stinky as we stood together in the huge pot-bellied cooking cauldron in an encampment of Bing-walla-walla pygmy tribesmen watching the bubbles begin to rise (Stinky's bowels are unreliable at the best of times, but stress makes them positively volcanic – "That'll ruin their soup!" I thought at the time, "And serve them right!"), it's not always easy to get hold of a sharpened pencil when you want one.

But now that we have arrived in something resembling civilization I thought it about time to send you a line or two, my old musk-rat.

Mind you, civilization is perhaps too grand a word to describe Hog's Spit Hollow, the little town in the outback of the Western Territories where we are currently residing. But they have a pub (always a plus) and that pub has something resembling a stage, so Stinky and I decided to revive our double act and bring a bit of culture to the dreary lives of the populace whilst at the same time trying to make a bob or two to enable us to patch up the old charabanc we are using as living accommodation and get on our way.

You remember our act, don't you my old furry-toed polecat? "Waiting for Sodo". Go on, you must remember. I kit myself out in a red wig and hussar's uniform, worn backwards and with the trouser legs rolled up to reveal green woollen socks and suspenders while Stinky, looking very laid back in a long blond hair piece, dons a Hawaiian shirt and taffeta knickerbockers. Luckily we always carry these around with us, along with our stage make-up – because you just never know when you've going to need it, do you?

Anyway, the curtain rises on Stinky and I sitting on a park bench with our backs to the audience. We go on to discuss weasels for a couple of hours before realising we'd never met one another before in our lives, haven't got a clue who on earth this mysterious Sodo feller is, nor even when he's supposed to be turning up, and that we have nothing all in common except for a love of the colour purple when used as a shadow nuance in Monet's early paintings. A case of mistaken identity coupled with a philosophical philippic on the relevance (or not) of all creatures stoatlike in the post-modern world. Gripping stuff, and just the sort of thing to wow your average outback sheep farmer, I would have thought.

But oddly enough it's not going down too well.

Mind you, the kind-hearted fellows are not wanting in their generous donation of provender throughout the performance. Most kind. We gather it all up at the end of the show, but I have to say that tomato soup and tomatoes on toast is getting a bit samey, if you know what I mean, Stinky not having much imagination in the culinary department, don't you know.

Still, on the bright side it seems that the populace have clubbed together and paid for the repairs on the old charabanc, so we can be on our way in a day or two. What larks!

Will drop you a line as soon as we find another stopping place. Love to all the sprogs, and give a cheery wave to all the other relatives.

Toodle pip

Great Uncle Horatius!"

I have to say that Ann did not greet Great Uncle H's missive with the wonder and awe that I expected, but rather much hooting and derisive scepticism saying that she didn't recall any relative, distant or not, called Horatius. She went on to say that she recalled me making up some stories about a Cousin Horatius when I was a child and that she rather thought I was dredging him up just to pad out my messages to her.

I was hurt. Mind you, dredging up is just the kind of thing one is likely to do with Great Uncle H, and he could well be both our uncle and cousin, or rather second cousin twice removed (due to the smell, but he keeps coming back). There was, so family rumour has it, a very delicate and embarrassing incident involving the Great H, his grandmother, a case of mistaken identity (not to be confused with a case of wine, which coincidentally, also came into the equation) and a prototype time machine discovered in a disused shed at the back of the local comprehensive school. Our cousin is therefore also our great uncle, but he is doing his best to hush up the whole affair. Unfortunately Stinky knows and holds the matter over poor Great Uncle H's head in a shameful and shameless manner, so that The Great H feels obliged to pay for Stinky's expenses on their various travels.

I think this (and the unfortunate bowel problem mentioned in GUH's missive) may be why he is referred to as Stinky.

Quite honestly I think that GUH's adventure quite put Ann's latest offering in the shade.

"Good morrow Ancient and Fetid One!" (*Upon reflection I think I prefer the Old Boot greeting*)

"Lam and I have just come back from our balloon flight! (OK, so we have also just come back from taking some rubbish to the dump, feeding Lam's sister and brother-in-law, sleeping, having breakfast three times and going to the loo (for details, refer to flow chart) but do we really need to be that precise? – We went on Friday morning) It were great!

There were twelve passengers and three staff, two to drive the Landrovers taking us to the launch pad and back from the swamp where we came down, and one pilot.

Now about the pilot. Did we tell you the moment of self-awareness when the Lam found out that he was a chauvinist? It was when we had boarded a very large plane and the pilot greeted us over the intercom and – it was a woman! There was much ribbing of Lamms when we got to our destination in the States and I let his consternation about being flown there by a woman be known to our hosts. All the ladies sharpened their knives and prepared to have barbequed Lam!

So you can imagine the Lam's phiz when this diminutive lady stepped forward and cheerfully announced:

'I will be your pilot today.'

All Chris had to say later on the subject was:

'I've only been flown twice by a woman, and half the times we crashed!' – But more of that later.

We all met in a busy Tesco car park just outside Plymouth and our pilot let off a small helium balloon to test the wind direction and, seeing that had we taken off from the car park we would have drifted over Plymouth (not advisable) or out to sea (also not advisable, coupled with the fact that there is not much landing opportunity unless an unwary basking shark had surfaced just at the crucial moment), we all piled into the Landrovers and headed out East to a disused airfield. She then sent up another small helium balloon and pronounced us good to go.

Then the fun started.

It's all down to 'spin', isn't it? Due to excellent advertising and psychology they actually got us to pay them to let us do most of the work of unrolling and spreading the envelope (balloon to you and me), hold it down while they filled it with cold and then hot air, and pile in. Think about it: they got paid for doing it and we paid them to let us do it. Someone somewhere must have read Tom Sawyer. I tried to suggest that Lam could have supplied all the hot air they needed for free, but was frowned down. We were then taught how to assume landing/crash positions (er, is it only me who sees something odd in the fact that landing and crash are used so synonymously??) - and we were off!

It seems strange to describe, but there was virtually no sense of rising or of being suspended approximately one mile high by nothing more than hot air and physics, and at that height it hardly felt like we were moving at all. In spite of a frosty morning it did not feel too cold (could have been either due to sunshine, in-house central heating/BBQ system, or just plain good old-fashioned six layers of clothing, pants and boots!). It was a beautiful, bright morning and we could see for miles. We saw over the Dartmoor moorlands, the coast from Dartmouth right down to Rame Head, Plymouth (thrills!) and many small towns and villages. Sheep, cows, trees, small patchwork fields, birds, ponds, sewage works – everything you could want.

The flight itself lasted about an hour, celebratory champagne was issued and then we slowly came down and our pilot looked for a place to land (she cannot steer, remember – 'Typical woman!' I hear coming from Chris) and we find that nearer to the land the breeze is stronger. We now do feel as if we are moving. A field is duly selected, we assume landing/crash positions – bounce, slide, bounce, long slide – and career gracefully into a hedge. And yes, that was considered a crash landing. It only happens about once in every nine hundred flights – heigh ho, what did we expect? Would probably have been just the same if we had had

Christopher-Robin aid the landing process with his pop gun! But we all agreed (all the passengers, that is, the other staff gave our pilot a hard time and the repairs will probably come out of her wages) that bouncing and sliding were absolutely great fun – especially the youngsters who were on the outside edge, but we oldies who were eventually dug out from inside the hedge also agreed (having removed the various leaves, twigs, spiders and stray sparrows from our hair and clothing) that it had indeed been great fun.

Our pilot then had to describe to the crew members who were sensibly following in the Landrovers where we were, and could they talk nicely to the farmer about his field (fortunately for the farmer it was a field of grass. Fortunately for the cows there were no cows in the field at the time, and fortunately for us it was not covered in cow-pats – now that would have given us a great slide!!)

Now lest you think that this is where we bid a cheerful farewell to our transport and crew – remember the advertising blurb under 'Frequently Asked Questions', and I quote: 'Can passengers participate in balloon inflation and deflation? (Like we are all panting to get involved) Answer: Absolutely! Passengers will be invited to assist the crew ......'

The fun thing about this flight was that, not only had we crashed into a hedge, but the balloon itself was draped over said hedge, over a small muddy lane, over another hedge and into another field (still mercifully non-crop, non-cow, non-cow-pat). The hedges were dear little Devon hedgerows with nice sharp branches, stinging nettles and nice prickly gorse bushes interwoven. Two of the girls managed to get themselves into the ditch completely enveloped by balloon, and no matter how they scrabbled, could not get themselves out. And the poor old balloon got ripped in two places as we all had to drag it over the nice spiky hedge.

We eventually packed it all away, the farmer was recompensed with complementary ticket and a bottle of wine, and off we went back to the car park where we were issued with certificates and Valium.

OK, forget all the moaning (which was, of course 'Merely corroborative detail, intended to give artistic verisimilitude to an otherwise bald and unconvincing narrative') we would not have missed it for worlds! It was a wonderful gift and a wonderful morning – thoroughly recommended.

Then we two went out for lunch at a little pub we just happened to notice as we flew over (we could *really* have 'dropped in'!) picked up our photographs, and went home.

Oh yes, and then we took our rubbish to the dump.

And went to the loo.

Etcetera.

Love twall

Mowl.

PS: Note seen on back of a sachet of rat poison: 'Warning: May contain nuts'. Someone asked the worrying question, 'What, you mean they make rat poison in a place where they also process nuts? Would they then have to put on the nuts: "Warning: may contain rat poison"? Or is the nut content considered of more concern than the rat poison? To persons other than the rat, that is.' My comment is: Nuts!!

PPS: I'm writing this at work and my boss says I should stop plaguing defenceless individuals (she doesn't know you) and get on with making the tea, that's what accounts (sorry, finance) departments are for, making tea, and cost it all out (including savings) while the kettle (bought cheap and put inventively through petty cash) is boiling, so I shall have to go (I just knew I'd reach the end of that sentence one day). I usually like to precede tea trips by saying: 'I'm going to the loo. Shall I fill the kettle?' But it doesn't go down very well."

Yes, I really think I shall have to dig out some more Great Uncle Horatius missives in order to compete with Ann's exciting lifestyle. It may be considered resorting to a sort of second cousin of Munchausen syndrome by proxy, but so what?

Chapter Seventeen

Took Arfer out for a walk this morning, and since Kester is away at the moment, Reeb had charge of Sophie. Because of both dogs' boisterous nature and penchant for flushing out pheasants or rabbits and chasing them to the distant horizon, I have invested in a couple of those extending leads. They wind out to sixteen feet and allow the dogs to trundle about in and out of ditches, round the odd tree (cue cursing) and into hedges. Arfer has various points along the way where he likes to check things out, like the gap in the hedgerow where the muntjac deer push through to drink at a stream, and the vole hole where he pushes his face right into the aperture and sniffs heavily and loudly. I fear that one day it will be a trip to the vet's to patch up vole scratches.

So the extending lead is a Good Thing for the dogs, but unfortunately it can make the walk a bit fraught for us, especially when Arfer, being of a substantial build, makes a sudden charge after something moving that takes his eye.

The first time I was alerted by the whizzing sound of the lead running out and I shouted out "Oh no!" as I realised I was standing on the edge of the stream filled ditch and Arfer had leapt to the other side and was diminishing fast. Luckily that time Reeb grabbed hold of me and we hauled the demi-rott back before I toppled into the mud.

The second time, however, I knew nothing until I was face down in the dirt half way through a hedge. A very surprised looking dog turned back to see what was impeding his progress.

It was also difficult because Arfer was so excited about having Sophie along for the walk as well that he leapt about like a wild thing, and every time Sophie stopped to sniff something, he hurtled at her, shoving his great big head down where she was investigating – sometimes with a really frightening crack as their skulls collided! – I don't know how little Sophie survived the impact! Anyway, as the walk progressed we had two excited dogs rushing about and around us, leads extending and retracting wildly, weaving in and out like maypole ribbons with Reeb and me as the poles! On more than one occasion Reeb and I suddenly found ourselves in a very intimate, if thrashing, embrace as we were knotted together and had to extricate ourselves, with great difficulty, shouting Vogonically at two dogs who couldn't see what all the fuss was about.

So it was not the most peaceful of walks and I lost count of the number of times I was nearly pitched into the watery ditch. I tried to persuade Reeb to walk on that side, but she would have none of it. So I was quite cheered when Sophie did an unexpected lurch and took her straight into the thorn hedge! Some very unmotherly chucklings ensued as a scowling Reeb limped home, plucking twigs and spiky bits out of her hair and clothing.

Back home Small reminded me that I had tentatively agreed to take the alpacas up to her lower school fete next Saturday. Apparently in a wild moment I had thought it might be fun to be a Feature of the fete with our brace of cameliads. I also thought that Others might share my excitement. I reckoned without the family recessive gloom gene nurtured so assiduously by my mother, May Hubbard, but which had skipped the female side of the family in my children's generation, and lodged itself firmly in my son.

Enthusiastically I told Kester of the Plans, and asked if he could possibly help (I must admit that the thought of just myself wrestling with fifty straw bales (to use as a pen), a hay net, a trug of water and two wilful alpacas was slightly daunting). The stare I got was one of horrified incredulity. The tirade I got would have been worthy of the Great Mother Hubbard in her stride.

What was I – stupid? – or had I just lost my mind? What was I thinking of, promising to take Dylan and Monty all that way – a full mile if it was an inch – without a horse box or trailer? Worse, what was I doing dragging Kester into My Problem?

I immediately backed down and decided that I would have to go by myself (Nic was away on business that weekend, Jay and Reeb were going to Alton Towers. Small wanted to help (bless), but, well, she's Small). I decided that it would be best if I had a practise run just to make sure I could actually walk the little blighters along the road, and Kester watched as I tried to corner the alpacas to put on their head collars. It was an impossible task for just one person. As soon as I got them near a corner of the field they would split up and bolt in opposite directions, leaving me floundering about like a fool. I'm sure they were playing with me because they allowed themselves to be herded right up to the fence, then they got a wild – perhaps even gleeful – look in their eyes and then charged! I felt very self-conscious dashing about like a wild thing as Kester watched, but eventually he took pity on me and he stumped over to help.

Of course as soon as he joined in the alpacas stopped their playing (sorry, I so-o-o-o wanted to write "sodding about", but of course I won't) and meekly allowed themselves to be caught. We put on the leads and took them through the gate and headed towards the village.

But it was no good.

They were both very spooked by the traffic, although everyone was very good, slowing right down to give us room ...... or possibly to stare in disbelief at the spectacle! Ann had recently regaled me with a poem she had written regarding a news item in her local paper where some alpacas had got loose:

A funny thing happened to me
On the road to Salisbury.
Cleaned my specs, thought that I had gone crackers!
For there on the road were mincing alpacas!

Well mine minced and spat and kicked! – and by the time we had gone a hundred yards or so (and I had received a number of very well placed kicks from Dylan) I decided it was no good, and we turned back.

Kester said not a word, but the lines of his back as he walked away from me had "I told you so" written all over them!

So I had to contact the school committee and tell them I couldn't get the alpacas up to the school. There was a flurry of phone calls as Annette (not one to give in easily when school events are involved) tried to borrow a horse trailer, but to no avail. I felt really bad.

There was great excitement the next evening as Kester announced that he was ready to start up the Diabolical Machine, and if we were very good he would let us watch. Jay came round with her video camera to film the event. The dogs were locked indoors, the hens rounded up and secured in their house, and the alpacas fitted with ear muffs. Neighbours were warned there may be the sound like Concorde passing over head, and friends were invited round for the occasion. A barbeque was lit and drinks passed round. Streamers hung from the trees and everything looked very merry.

To the braying of trumpets the Diabolical Machine was wheeled out and took centre stage in the floodlit garden. We were all ordered to stand at a safe distance ("Behind the tape, please. And are you sure Emma-Lee should be out here, Mum? Oh all right, but put these darkened glasses on her, will you?") and Kester walked forward to connect the make-shift fuel tank cunning devised from an old plastic orangeade bottle, and a hush fell on the assembled crowd. He bent over the Diabolical Machine and fiddled with something. The hush grew more intense. He called for a screwdriver and a speculative whisper susserated through the crowd.

There was more fiddling.

Then more fiddling.

There was a sort of "phutt" accompanied by a very swift, dull red glow, the plastic bottle promptly melted and spilled fuel down the front of Kester's trousers, a crowded few seconds as Kester beat out the small flame that leapt from the dull red glow onto his saturated trousers, and finally a very red-faced, slightly smoking, Kester turned to the crowd and announced that there would now follow a short recess.

Of about two months.

Apparently something had been fitted the wrong way round and it will require complete stripping down to put it right. But since Kester is now suffering Huge Humiliation the Diabolical Machine (after being given a hearty kick) has been wheeled back into the barn by a limping Owlmaster, and I fear will not see the light of day for some time.

Nic's mother, Greechie (aged ninety-eight) had come over for the occasion, but had fallen asleep in her chair by the fire and so missed it. As we settled ourselves in the room around her she roused herself with a loud yawn, looked across to Nic and commented, very loudly:

"I've never seen you in mauve before."

Nic was sitting there in jeans and a green tee-shirt ……

It rounded off a very exciting day to find that I had an e-mail from Ann.

"Wot Ho to the Old Boot!

'How I Cleared All the Crocodiles Out of the River Zambezi And Still Had Time To Cook Tea (or: Wot I Dun at the Weekend)'.

Perhaps it is a wee bit boastful of me to claim that I cleared *all* the crocs out of the Zambezi. Actually I only cleared the grinning toothful ones from my little stretch of the river. After it had been diverted our way by the Monsoon that swept across the continents, along the Gulf Stream and up the River Tamar.

That was Saturday.

The morning was fine and dry with no hint of What Was to Come. I mooched about in the garden, eyeing up the shrubbery that was making a bid to take over the house and swallow it up in a verdant mass of rustling, inexorably creeping greenery. I dug out my machete, whetted it carefully on a dampened stone, packed up a rucksack of fresh water, beef jerky, a piece of Kendal cake and a Werther's Original, kissed the cat goodbye, and then, singing 'It's a Long Way to Tipperary' to keep my spirits up, I hacked my way into the undergrowth, slashing and burning in good Amazon Rain Forest style. The burgeoning greenery closed about me, swallowing me up and sucking me deeper and deeper into its pulsing dark bosom.

Gad but it was dark in there!

Luckily I was equipped with pit-helmet and safari clothes and was able to take evasive action when the first anaconda dropped out of the trees and across my shoulders. With a deft swipe of my machete I lopped the head off the evil-eyed, hissing devil, and taking the rest of the monstrous body by the tail I swung it around just in time to ward off the tiger that, burning brightly, was creeping through the undergrowth towards me, a fiercesome snarl curling the black lips away from its cruelly gleaming teeth.

Trembling a little now, and disorientated by the sight of the tiger, I turned back to the jungle path I had been clearing. I wiped the sweat from my eyes and proceeded, all the while watching out for more dangers. A troop of monkeys hung in the branches of the viburnum tinus, watching me with beady little eyes, picking fruit off the snowberry bush and lobbing them at me half-heartedly. I was so busy watching them that I did not see the giant spider's web looped between two Torbay palms until I was caught in its sticky, clinging embrace. I struggled wildly, slashing with my machete, desperately trying to break free as I saw the leaves part and an enormous spider begin to drag its swollen, hairy abdomen across the ground towards me, it's front legs groping about ahead of it like a blind man's white stick, feeling, feeling, coming ever closer!

At that moment a guinea fowl burst unexpectedly onto the scene, squawking and clattering madly, flapping her wings and sending speckled feathers twirling into the air like an exploding pillow. She cannoned into me, just giving me enough impetus to break the last web-threads that held me, and together the guinea fowl and I fell sprawling into a white flowered hebe. Grateful to the little bird I picked her up, kissed her on the beak, reached for a hanky to staunch the flow of blood from the peck she gave me in response, tucked her under my arm, and set off on my way. I was happier now I knew that at least dinner was taken care of (it's funny how sentimentality can be washed away by a bit of wounding).

On we went, deeper and deeper into the undergrowth. It grew darker. I was sure I could hear the sound of distant drums. But I was mistaken. It was thunder!

All of a sudden the heavens opened and rain lashed down upon us as a mighty wind roared about us, ripping leaves off the bushes, bending trees over until their trunks groaned almost to breaking point. The little bird was ripped from my grip and went spiralling away, caught up in a tornado inside of which I'm sure I caught sight of a lion, a scarecrow and a robot – or maybe it was a tin man, I can't be certain. I gave a little cry as she went, but I knew there was nothing I could do.

For now I had to worry about myself. Rain rushed and roared about my head. Water rushed and roared about my legs, pulling at me so that I had to grip onto a passing log in order to save myself from being swept along by the current. It was as I was hanging onto the log, however, that I suddenly realised that it was not a log but a crocodile! It was the muddy waters of the Zambezi that roiled and boiled about my knees, and now crocodiles were snapping at me, chewing on spider and tiger and eyeing me up for dessert!

It was a wild hour or so, I can tell you! I fought my way through the lashing rain, burst out from the undergrowth onto the main road beyond, and there I stood, the Monsoon drenching me, falling so hard that I could hardly open my eyes because my eyelashes were sodden and heavy. Gasping, I tried to get air through the liquid atmosphere. Desperately, blindly, I reached down into the raging brown waters and groped around. At last I found what I was searching for and I heaved with all my might until at last the invading Zambezi swirled into the gaping hole. Crocodiles went spinning and snapping, trying to grip onto the sides of the manhole with their pathetic little feet, hesitating, trembling on the brink until at last they were ripped away with the tide to be swept down, down, down to the sewers and off to Plymouth. There they would join all the other crocodiles and alligators that had been flushed away by owners who had bought cutsy little baby reptiles and then got frightened as they grew, and grinned at them knowingly through the Perspex of their tanks.

Finally, the last crocodile gone, I fell into the water, my eyes closed, gasping and trembling with exertion, giving thanks for the fact that I was alive and, for the moment, safe.

But I gave my thanks too soon. I was roused from my stupor by a strange sound, a loud bleating, honking sound. I sat up and saw a great monster with glowing yellow eyes leering down at me, almost upon me. I leapt up, blinked the rain from my eyes, groping for the machete that had been lost in the raging flood, determined to muster the last of my strength and fight off this new and dreadful foe. Then I realised it was Lam in his car tooting the horn and leaning out of the window asking me what the devil I thought I was doing lying out in the road in the rain?

So we went in for a cup of tea, and for some reason Chris would not believe me about the snake and the spider and tiger and monkeys and crocodiles ...... some people have no imagination.

TRANSLATION:

On Saturday I had a go at taming the shrubs out in the front garden, but suddenly a strong wind blew up, soon to be followed by a tremendous cloud burst that dumped about an inch of rain in an hour on Saltash. So I stopped and had to go indoors.

Put that in Great Uncle Horatius's pipe and ask him to smoke it!

Love twall

A Lightly Dampened Mowl

PS: Lam is disappointed. Lam is weeping. Lam has invaded Eeyore's gloomy corner and is mumbling disconsolately. Lam is not impressed.

Fanfare? BBQ? Marching alpaca band? Hen juggling?

Yea, everything you could possibly want for the big unveiling of the Diabolical Machine except it's Chief Champion – Uncle Lam!!

Shame on that Owlmaster and a pestilence upon his house! No wonder it went 'phutt'. With Lam adding his little mite of tinkering you could have had a mushroom cloud! Demons could have been dragged screaming from the pits! (ie: the girls roused from their beds). The earth could have been broken asunder and dimensions breached! Demi-rottweilers could have been launched! You could have found yourself (mounted aboard an alpaca, hen under arm (saves on deodorant) and Small clutched to your bosom) orbiting Mars!

But, no. You gathered together in a little huddle and plotted.

'Ban the Lam' you said.

'We have a Boy and a Diabolical Machine, we do not need a Lam,' you said.

'Synergy (sin + energy),' you said.

And so you had a phutt. And you deserve it.

PPS: An alpaca went off to the fete

To join in the fun with his mate
He went down real big
With his soft fleece and wig
And the numerous sprogs that they ate!

PPPS: Ooo, just thought of another one:
'Alpacas!' cried Small, 'To my class!'
But the trek up the road was a farce.
They ran for their pens
And trampled the hens
And kicked my poor Sis on the side of her ankle bone!"

I'm sorry that Chris's nose has been put out of joint because of not being invited to the failed inauguration of the Diabolical Machine. But what was all that about crocodiles and tigers in Saltash??? – I feel a competition in the imagination stakes coming on ......

(It will be noticed that I am choosing to ignore the so-called literary offerings. I think it's for the best)

Chapter Eighteen

Well, I just can't let Ann get away with her last e-mail without some kind of response. So it's back to the Great Uncle Horatius archives, I think.

As luck would have it I had just received a postcard from the aged relative giving me the latest up-date on his exploits and (just by-the-way) informing me of his overseas bank account number so that I could wire him some money which he said he needed rather desperately. At first I thought it was some sort of ransom, but now it seems it is to enable him to bribe some border guards and hire a small skiff capable of negotiating the mangrove swamps of Papua New Guinea.

It seems that he and Stinky were in a shady bar in downtown Jakarta, throwing back banana daiquiris with lime vodka chasers and playing a game of strip mah-jong with a group of burly Lascar sailors when Stinky decided that he didn't like the look of one of the ratings, and slipped him the card of a back-street cosmetic surgeon he was friendly with. He added, with a wink, that after the attentions of the surgeon, a decent haircut, and with a bit of a wardrobe make-over plus some kindly lighting, the fellow could look almost human, if one ignored the hump. The chap to whom this friendly advice was directed also happened to be deaf, and so smiled and nodded politely.

The other sailors, however, not only heard, but had only a scant knowledge of English, especially when spoken with a daiquiri slurred Etonian accent. They therefore leaped to the conclusion that Stinky was making very improper suggestions to their comrade, and in a moment there was the flash of teeth and steel in the flickering lamplight, and if GUH hadn't had the presence of mind to grab the still benignly smiling Stinky by his shirt collar and haul him out of his chair, it would have been his spine shattered by the machete instead of the chair back.

In the uproar that followed, GUH and Stinky nipped smartly into a back storeroom of the bar and hid. Everything would have been all right if they had just managed to lay low until the bar room brawl had subsided and the shouting Lascars departed, but Stinky made the mistake of lighting a match to see where exactly they were – and if any alcohol, and possibly a few peanuts, were available to hand to while away the next couple of hours. He was just mouthing out the words "Danger, fireworks" which was written in faded letters on the box in front of him, when the still-lighted match dropped from his hand.

GUH didn't have much to say about the next few minutes, indeed his writing became a little wobbly as he was apparently overcome by emotion at the memory. He did mention something about the smell of burning hair and how surprisingly cold a Jarkartan night can be when you're completely naked and gently smoking from persistent magnesium embers, but it was all a bit stilted.

Anyway, it seems that as they staggered out of the smoke they were confronted by the sight of the Lascars, the irate owner of the erstwhile bar (who was jumping up and down shaking his fists and demanding reparation for the loss of his building, his fireworks and his trade), a jeep full of soldier who appeared to be very eager to manhandle a couple of foreigners, and a strange, buxom, shrieking woman with vibrant red hair who had apparently appeared from nowhere and whose appearance made Stinky turn pale beneath the soot and leg it up an alley with the agility of a gazelle with the smell of lion in its nostrils, with no word of warning to GUH.

GUH was suddenly alone, naked, back up against a wall with a mob baying for his blood converging upon him with the swift inexorability of a herd of stampeding wildebeest. Quick as a flash GUH held up his hand and bellowed "Stop!" as loudly as he could, and, strangely enough, they did. Then, with great aplomb, the old buzzard asked if anyone had a hanky they could lend him as he felt a sneeze coming on, and as the crowd murmured to one another and patted their pockets in search of a handkerchief, GUH strolled through them and would have made his escape had not the buxom red-haired woman taken his wrist in a vicelike grip as he passed her and demanded in a thick, heavily-accented voice:

"You are friend of the one they call – Putrid?"

GUH was so taken by this new name for Stinky that instead of breaking free and making a dash for it, he hesitated. And so was lost.

Jarkartan jails, so I am reliably informed by my esteemed relative, are not places you should rush to book yourself into for any period of time. They are small. They are hot. They smell. And there are rats. Rats so big that on a dark night they could be mistaken for small ponies. Rats so bold that when you are thrown into the cell they glance up at you from the newspaper they are reading, lying back at leisure on the hard bench that is the bed, and merely yawn. Rats, in fact, that you would really rather not meet under any circumstances, and certainly not stark naked, smelling enticingly of singed flesh, and in a confined space.

The handwriting of the Great Uncle wobbled again. I believe I even detected a tear stain. But all this, you will be pleased to know, has a Happy Ending. Or at least, an Ending – and having struggled through so much of this tedious narrative, that must surely count as being Happy.

Two nights later, as GUH was writing out yet another IOU to a big black rat smoking a bad cigar and gleefully shuffling a dog-eared pack of cards, there came through the barred window of the cell the distinctive smell of dodgy eau de cologne and cheap brandy. GUH leaped to his feet and, daring not to believe his nostrils, warbled out a few bars of "Father Hold the Candle While I Shave the Chicken's Lip", then waited with bated breath as the thick Jakarta night pressed in around him. After a moment there was a hiccup and then an answering rendition of "Treacle, Peas and Small Fat Fleas Fill Weasel Dreams At Dusk" wafted in on the breeze followed, unexpectedly, by a lot of shushing, a small belch and the unmistakable giggle of a woman.

Stinky (and friend) had come to the rescue!

It was but the work of a week or so before the bars at the prison window were finally removed and GUH hauled to relative safety by Stinky and the buxom red-haired woman. Bidding a fond farewell to the Big Black Rat and promising to be back within the year with the stock shares and the deeds to his Portuguese maize plantation in order to settle his gambling debts, GUH, Stinky and the buxom red-haired woman slipped off into the night.

Stinky had thoughtfully brought with him a big black beard and sunglasses for GUH to use as a disguise, but, unhappily, no clothes. GUH experimented with the wig to see if it could be used to ensure his modesty rather than wrap around his face, but the results were startling rather than reassuring, and the idea had to be abandoned. However, when they had gone a couple of miles they came upon suburban civilization, and a quick washing-line snatch provided a pair of purple frilly knickers, disconcertingly tied at the sides with orange ribbon, a gold-edged vermilion sarong and a rather fetching flower print blouse two sizes too small for him. And with these GUH had to be satisfied as Stinky, having ditched the buxom red-haired woman once and for all, hustled him along the alleyways to the port where they stowed away on a battered little steamboat outward bound for Australia.

Unfortunately Stinky and GUH were discovered as

they raided the ship's galley one night in search of pink gin and crudités, and they were put off the boat at Papua New Guinea.

GUH had to sign off then, having run out of space on his postcard, but he promises he will write again soon to tell me about the Curious Incident of the Small Pink Pig in the Night and Stinky's engagement. Riveting stuff.

Another evening, another e-mail from Ann.

"Greetings Trout in Boots!" (*ah, so now she's going for mixed insults. I can take it. My back is broad*) "(Rather think that would make a good pantomime, that, Trout in Boots. The trout could be the main character, cunningly inserted into boots somehow, perhaps strapped to the tail fins, or maybe the main character (principal boy or girl – or possibly even the Dame) could have the trout in their boots with all the hilarity that would ensue from such a predicament. I shall work on a script and see what you think)

How's your garden looking at the moment? Ours is a bit disappointing. Most of the little plants I put in did not survive the summer. They drowned. And the lawn cannot be walked upon as it is so soggy. However, you will be pleased to know that the algae on the patio is thriving wonderfully.

Anyway, you may remember (if you are any kind of loving and concerned sister, which is doubtful from the messages of glee I receive when I reach out for sympathy after having a cold, or slicing my thumb open and having to contend with a rubber glove for a week or so) that I have been having trouble with my stomach. Well, Lam suggested that I go and get tested for food intolerance. Personally I thought this was going to be a waste of time and that they would say 'None whatsoever' and I could say 'Told you so' to Lam and then tuck into a nice fat juicy cake to celebrate.

Should've known better.

I must say I was prepared for the announcement of a wheat intolerance, and was not overly surprised to learn of my system's dislike of cow's milk products – I even nodded sadly when onions were mentioned. However, when it came to oats, rye, mixed pollens (of course),mixed weed/shrub (lightly boiled), prawns (only mildly), tomatoes (only mildly), monosodium glutamate (only mildly), CHOCOLATE and RED WINE!! – Wail! For some reason she did not mention white wine (I wisely did not point this omission out and question it, but take it as a green light signal). Since wine (or at least red wine) was mentioned I did wonder if I had an intolerance to grapes in general ...... but I think that query can be shelved (wouldn't you??)).

So, OK, I'm a big girl (rapidly getting smaller after all those prohibitions!) I can handle this. Mumble, grumble. Breakfast: fruit, OK, I suppose. Lunch in special recipe pancakes, OK. Dinner: meat, potatoes and veg, OK. Well, not so bad then, I thought, cheering up.

But oh no, of course things are never that simple, are they? Evidently the lady I consulted was a sadist disguised as a nutritionist and she further added that I should also avoid yeast (Oxo cubes, so no gravy to hit the chop!) and try this food combining system (Hay Diet? – Heard of it?). So do not have protein and carbohydrates together like: fish and chips; chilli and rice (I can have it with lentils, not rice. Yeah, right!); roast beef and Yorkshire pudding; jacket potatoes with cheese – and more or less anything you might fancy. In fact any normal meal. Wail again!

The probiotic tablets I accept.

All of this, however, pales into insignificance beside the linseed oil. I innocently went home vowing to eat my seeds and cucumber on lettuce leaf and to take my probiotic tablets and linseed oil ......

Then I tried the linseed oil. ......!!!

It tastes like something you put on furniture! It is horrendous! You swallow it, apply superhuman control not to gag, then quickly stuff your sawdust and birdsdropping – oh, sorry, non-gluten meusli to you – down your gob and swallow hard.

The trouble is, it repeats! Burp, groo! Burp, groo!

Someone said I could make a salad dressing with it and put it all over our dinner. I said I valued my marriage too highly and looked wonderingly at her – has she tried it?? A quick spoonful is bad enough, never mind a slow enjoyment of the full flavour all over your dinner!

Drizzle (n) Wot we have a lot ov in Cornwall

Drizzle (v) To precipitate lightly on edible matter. Origin: probably Cornwall (where they drizzle for England). Uses: olive oil salad dressing on feta cheese salad pancake wrap. Result: a happy Mowl. Non-uses: linseed oil on salad or said Mowl. Result: sleek but wrathful Mowl. Useful warning: Don't mess wiv de Mowl.

No doubt life will be worth living again sometime.

Having shelled out considerable mullah for the consultation, and a steamer, I will of course give the diet a go. However, I do not intend to be a pain (well, no more than usual) when visiting people. I shall just smile and say 'Thank you for my dinner' – unless, of course, it's linseed soup – and sort my guts out later.

I bought myself a new dress for going out in the evening. Assuming we can find restaurants with a menu that covers my new diet. Or one where the chef makes imaginative use of linseed oil in his recipes (thinks: would I *want* to dine at such a restaurant???). I was tempted by feathers and sequins, but had to settle for lots and lots of blue ruches and ruffles.

I feel like a cake.

Making a cake of myself?

– Which sadist mentioned cake?!

I hope you are all well. If not, I can recommend a diet. You can have it any time. Just ask. I will even send you my linseed oil.

Love twall
Melancholy Mowl

PS: Helen at work informs me that she gives linseed oil to

her horses one week before a show and it makes their coats lovely and glossy. I expect to be much admired.

PPS: Re the Diabolical Machine: Did you hear Lam and the Owlmaster colluding last night? Those malefacting males were discussing unspeakable things on the phone! I distinctly heard Lam suggesting the benefits of using a converted pony (air) bottle. But I'm not sure what for. Guard well your hens!

Love
Melancholy (but shiny) Mowl"

Chapter Nineteen

Had a message from Marie bemoaning the fact that she had been caught by a speed camera for going at 34 miles per hour in a 30 zone. I sent her a comforting message back saying that we are all OK with the knowledge that we now have a convicted felon in our midst and hope that she gave them a run for their money since we do like a good car chase. I requested that she let me have her vital statistics so that I could knit her a jumper with black arrows over it with a lovely matching ball and chain for her ankle. Small wanted to send her a "Get out of jail free" card from her Monopoly set, but I said that (regretfully) that doesn't work in the real world. Reeb was very concerned as well and got busy looking for recipes for a cake with a file in it, but couldn't find a suitable one. I was rather uncharitable and mentioned that she didn't need to add the file, her cakes tend to be so "substantial" that all Marie would need to do would be to lob it at the guard when he opened her cell door and it would knock him out cold, and Marie could then make good her escape.

No doubt at this point we could enlist Rugg, suitably attired in mobster suit and leather driving gloves, to be sitting outside the prison revving the engine waiting for her ...... although knowing Rugg he would probably be waiting outside the wrong prison looking confused (remember the verb to Rugg? – to bumble about in vague fashion wondering what you are doing here in the first place).

It was a disappointment to discover that no criminal prosecution was to be forthcoming, nor even any points on the licence as Marie was instead offered the option of going back to school to take a class on being a Good Driver and to watch some hair-raising film showing ghastly crashes and mutilations resulting from speeding accidents.

I hope Marie behaves. No sitting at the back of the class giggling and flicking ink pellets at the heads of those in front of her.

Small is developing the family skill of sarcasm, I am slightly ashamed to say. Reeb was tidying her room on Friday and found she had nowhere to put her fish tank, so she foolishly went into Small's room while she was at school and removed a little table upon which the tank fitted quite neatly.

That evening Small came home, stood in her doorway looking at the empty space and became quite (justifiably) annoyed that her sister had taken something of hers without asking. Later (having apparently given the problem much thought) she went into Reeb's room and asked airily:

"Reeb, do you know where I can get hold of a table the same size and shape that *that* one?" – pointing at her own table.

Reeb was suitably abashed.

I hear that Ann and Chris are doing a spot of decorating in their house. Ann has been assigned the en suite bathroom to paint, which I think could be a mistake. I get the feeling that merely sloshing on a coat of magnolia emulsion is not in her style. There could be a lot of colour going into that small room, or, memories of her balloon flight still lingering, she could well be dreamily painting fluffy white clouds upon the cerulean shades I know Chris had in mind.

Actually, a mural might not be a bad idea. Give them something to focus on when meditating after a particularly rich dinner, or an inadvertent overdose of linseed oil. She could go classical and paint colonnades at each side of the wall with a rustic landscape across which toga-clad images of herself frolic through the grass and daisies pursued by saturnine Lams – the goats' legs would be most appropriate! Or she could paint a life-sized, photographically detailed representation of Chris (possibly naked, but preferably not) standing right behind the door to surprise (or shock) people when they use their facilities ...... oh, it's their en suite she's decorating ...... then perhaps that might be an idea for another room. Anyway, anything would be better than the mirror that Jay has for some reason decided would be a Good Thing to position in front of her toilet. There is *nothing* more off-putting than seeing yourself going purple faced from a good strain when you need to concentrate!

Actually, mirrors at my time of life are not a good thing anywhere in the house. All right, so you need one just to check that you look basically neat before venturing out into the wide world – you know, that your hair isn't sticking out as though doing an impersonation of an abandoned thrush's nest, or that your skirt isn't hooked into your knickers (been there, done that – don't want the tee-shirt, thank you very much!), but no longer do I want one a) over the bath, b) anywhere I plod first thing in the morning, or c) anywhere near a toilet. The best place for a mirror is on the inside of a wardrobe door, covered with a sheet so that I don't startle myself when I go to fetch out clothes.

I've been thinking about something Ann told me about her possibly having caught sight of the Beast of Bodmin. I wonder if Chris is measuring up a space on the wall to have the head stuffed and mounted, like the gnu (but not the dreadful hearty beast, oh gno, gno, gno)?

Personally I do not believe in the Beast. I think it is all a con by Saltash district council, but I'm not quite sure what the con is. Perhaps, a) it's a way of enticing more tourists down across the bridge in order to relieve them of their dosh with guided tours of The Beast's haunts, or selling postcards with shadowy pictures of the alleged Beast, plaster casts of its paw prints and plastic toys (with pop-out fangs and bulging eyes) for the kiddies, or b) a way of scaring tourists into *not* coming across The Bridge and therefore keeping Kernow for the Kernowish (?).

It could be either. Or a bit of both. I'm not sure.

At home all has gone very quiet re the Diabolical Machine. I am happy with the silence. Let sleeping boats lie; don't question the dog; ask no rocks; etcetera, etcetera.

Rugg phoned today. He didn't mean to, but he did. There was a lot of wind, the shushing of trouser material on leg and a muffled conversation apparently between Rugg and a car mechanic. After bellowing down the phone several times in an attempt to get my father's attention to alert him to the fact that his pocket was making a rather expensive telephone call without his knowledge, I went to put the phone down and wait for the line to clear. However, I was suddenly intrigued as I noted the exasperated tone of the mechanic explaining, very carefully and slowly, that although Rugg might indeed have successfully used an old baked bean tin to repair a hole in an exhaust pipe thirty or so years ago, he (the mechanic) had no knowledge of any modern equivalent, low cost solution to Rugg's current car problem and that the £107 he wanted to charge was not a "rip off".

I mentally wished the mechanic good luck and went upstairs to fire up the computer and read Ann's latest offering.

"Greetings Fish Face," (*so we're back to the piscine insults, are we? I do feel my sister could be more inventive*)

"Well, not a lot has been happening here recently. We have had a prolonged break from work due to lack of orders, so I got out a nice big toilet roll and proceeded to make a List of Things To Do for both Chris and myself.

Then I went sick.

It was an odd sort of flu-y bug which rendered the bug-ee absolutely exhausted. One week gone. Then, just as I was starting to feel better and to reach out one wasted paw for my list, I sprained my wrist*. It is extremely infuriating and awkward (difficult is probably overstating it a bit) trying to do things with one hand – and this time a rubber glove could not make life a little easier, or at least interesting.

Typing? – Hmmm, soon starts to ache.

Decorating? – ha!

Washing up? – Come hither little Lam!

General housework? – grump, grump. Some, unfortunately.

But gardening? – Phoooooeeey!

Pulling up your drawers? – Baggy is *in*, man! I mean, like, really me!!

But I can (and do) spit feathers. I shall probably be fine by the time I get the call to go back to work, but in the mean time the calendar flicks over and the house remains the same. Grump!

*OK Grot Bag, you win! – I was hoping to slip in that little comment about a sprained wrist in the middle of talking about doing things one-handed in the hopes that you would be so taken up with sisterly sorrow and reaching for the keyboard in order to write a letter of condolence and sympathy that the old basilisk eye would not notice the actual spraining of the wrist, and therefore not demand an accounting.

Sigh. It was all very embarrassing.

No, that is not a particularly shepherd-warning sunset you are experiencing, it is the glow from the Mowl's cheeks as she recalls the events!

I was just starting to feel better after the flu-y thing and was doing a particularly Mowline salsa around the kitchen (with Billy Joel pumping out 'Don't Ask Me Why' on the CD player) as I prepared dinner for our friends Kevin and Deb. Soon we were joyously arranged around the table when I leapt up to fetch something (as you do), dropped my napkin on the wooden floor, stepped on it and – whoooooosh! – slithered through into the lounge where I came to an abrupt halt, slamming down on bot and wrist! Immediately leapt up with a very embarrassed 'Oops, silly me!' and continued as if nothing had happened, even though I felt that horrible swimming sensation that usually presages a faint, and had to sit quietly in the kitchen out of sight of our guests for a few minutes to let it pass.

Next day my wrist was almost unmoveable, so I was hauled up to St Barnabas' (local Saltash A&E) for a quick check over, expecting a kiss-it-better style bandage and a lecture on not being such a clumsy clutz. But instead I got:

'Ooo, I'm not sure about that. Reckon you'll 'ave to go over to Liskeard to 'ave 'im checked out.'

St Barnabas' is very good, but so 'local' that they have no x-ray facility, and, guess wot? – Liskeard has no fracture clinic and so would have had to refer me to Derriford Hospital in Plymouth.

Why St Barnabas' could not send me dreckly to Derriford can only be understood by locals – certainly not by me. But never mind! I sort of *knew* it wasn't broken, so was happy to settle for Liskeard, which would probably not have much in the way of queues and was, anyhow, expecting me (the nurse having telephoned to ask their expert opinion on an injury they could not see). I have lost track of this paragraph. Never mind, you have probably lost the will to live after reading all this, and so have I.

Let it just be said that, following four x-rays, I was despatched back to minor injuries with a little piece of card with NBI on it (I am ashamed to say that my thoughts as to what NBI stood for lapsed into Australian possibilities) and was issued with a tight 'sock' with my thumb sticking out and a sheet of instructions on how to cope with a poorly wrist. I made a thorough search and nothing was said about husbands and washing up. What kind of instructions do you call that?!

Now. As you know, this is Britain. And it comes to my mind that the Health and Safety Executive may get involved here. This could well mean that in future, any time I wish to

---

issue guests with napkins, I may be required to run a Risk Assessment and issue a Method Statement!

Let me forestall them.

Risk Assessment:

There is evidence that members of the public may be subjected to a slip or trip hazard whilst operating fabric/paper napkins in the vicinity of hardwood flooring and whilst using feet, knees, hands or other mode of propelling themselves in a variety of directional movements across said hardwood flooring.

Method Statement:

Hardwood flooring may be removed and replaced with non-slip carpeting. Napkins may be embroidered/printed with large red letters to the effect:

Warning!

May cause slip or trip hazard when dropped/left on hard surface and stepped on!

Should napkin inadvertently be dropped, the whole area should be fenced or coned off and large notices erected with the same warning as on the napkin. Or we could dispense with tables, plates, knives, forks, spoons and (especially) napkins and all stick our faces in a trough in the middle of the floor!!

Woja fink?

But we are now improving and the list is once more clutched in the wasted paw. Lam suggested that we (at last) put up the blind in the new(ish) kitchen and I began skipping around with joy (having only mentioned it thirty or forty times in the past two months!) and then remembered how it had been when we did the blind in the bedroom. Skipping ceased and I made a dive for my wrist 'sock', mewing piteously that it was too weak for me to get involved.

Hah! I should have saved the tears!

We measured, re-measured, discussed, argued, measured again, paused for tea and sustenance, measured it, spread it all out on the lounge floor, measured again, discussed it, and then Lam cut the tube to size. Then we measured it again and congratulated ourselves on Stage One being successfully completed.

Now to cut the fabric.

This is Mowl's job.

Problem No. 1 (in fact the whole problem as far as I was concerned!): Lam does not give up control without a fight, a lecture, much soul searching and an eagle eye on every twitch of an eyelash! The blind was duly measured. It was marked. There was a lecture on how the marking should take place with Lam hovering over the fabric with his micrometer (yes, his micrometer. 'You are .453mm out between the first and last marks'!!). There was a lecture on what I was leaning on. There was a lecture on which way round the measuring stick should go. There was a lecture on how to draw the line.

Then Lam drew the line.

Then I cut.

Lam made me a nice bold line which can still be seen on the blind, and I am extremely concerned that I could have stayed perfectly within the bounds of said line and still have been .0456328mm out between the start and end of it.

Question: Should I own up? Is it worth buying a new blind over?

The blind is up and I have gone to lie down in a darkened room with a damp towel over my eyes.

Lotsa luv
Mowl"

Actually, my sympathies were with Ann and her DIY

experience. Nic is a very willing DIY-er. Eager to please, uncomplaining. But not very good.

I recently wanted some book shelves put up in the living room. Firstly I approached Kester who (to my surprise) agreed. He put up two shelves in an alcove beside the fireplace over the television set. They are perfect. Well, not actually perfect because apparently they are .452mm out, like Ann's blinds, and the engineering Owl threw down his tools in self-disgust, made me swear that I would not tell anyone, especially any other men, that he had put them up, and declared loudly and in a manner that would brook no argument that he was not going to put up the other three shelves I wanted because he was No Good at it and it would torture him to look at them and see such a disgustingly and inaccurately executed job was down to him.

So Nic put them up, with my help.

Like Ann and Chris, we measured, we discussed, we measured again. We retreated for cups of tea and sustenance, then returned to re-measure. We marked the wall. We measured again. Nic drilled the holes. I held the spirit level. We stood back and made a visual assessment of the marks, squinting and measuring them against ceiling and wall. We congratulated each other on a job well done, screwed the shelves to the wall, placed a pencil onto the shelf ...... and watched in dismay as it rolled from one end to the other, gathering an impressive amount of speed as it went.

Upon re-measuring we were both amazed to find that our shelves were in fact two whole inches out!!

Neither of us could understand it.

Kester does not mention them.

Chapter Twenty

Had to check my clock this morning because it was so pitch black that I thought it was still night instead of seven o'clock in the morning. Tried to lever Small out from her pit, which was no mean task. I think she had managed to molecularly integrate herself into the fabric of her duvet.

We had hail today, really heavy and prolonged. Went outside to see if it hurt to be hit by the hail. It did.

And that is very sad.

Luckily I had another missive from the old Relic today, so perhaps I can pass that on to Ann in lieu of anything deep and interesting in my life. I'm so happy to see him and Stinky on good terms again after that dreadful occasion some years ago when there was a bit of a fracas between GUH and Stinky, something about a disputed fiancée they suddenly found they shared in common, and a small matter of an IOU for £3,000 made out to Stinky which appeared to be in GUH's handwriting, but which he could not remember penning, and they had parted company on very bad terms. However, some months later there was a very emotional, not to say maudlin, reunion – at Maudlin College, Oxford, funnily enough.

GUH was going through maps of the lesser known regions of Borneo wither he was next bound, when he looked up and caught sight of Stinky thumbing through a first edition Lolita. Their eyes met, there was a tense moment, then they rushed together and there was much falling upon necks and weeping and begging of forgiveness all round. It all got very messy. Especially as the security guards followed them to the pub whence they had retired to drink each other's good health, and frisked Stinky for the first-edition which, in his delight at finding GUH again, he had inadvertently slipped in his inside pocket instead of back in its glass cabinet.

Anyway, it appears that everything turned out all right, and it seems that they are off on their travels again, although not, it transpires, to Borneo.

"Wot Ho me Proud Beauty!" (*he wrote*)

Just wanted to thank you for the supply of wonga you so generously wired me care of Ali's Gin and Dance Emporium in Cairo. It couldn't have come at a better time! Performing the Dance of the Seven Veils each night to a drunken, raucous, knife-bearing audience is not something I'd recommend as a career option, especially when you shed the final bit of gauze and see the looks of disappointment in their eyes. Mind you, a look of bitter disappointment is infinitely better than the gleam of interest you sometimes get, and on more than one occasion I've had to use the old silver tongue to get out of a sticky situation. I mentioned my discomfort to Old Stinky and he suggested that I left the disrobing to him while I added a bit of counterpart to the drums on my ukulele. I was getting a bit worried about poor old Stinky who was beginning, I fear, to enjoy it a tad too much.

But your spot of dosh enabled us to pay off the black-hearted blaggard who held our charabanc hostage, stock up with a few provisions from the local offy, and high tail it out of the land of the Pharaoh's lickety split.

And so, deciding to shake the dust of Egypt off our feet (quite literally) we now find ourselves in much cooler climes. Indeed we had to trade our charabanc (plus three bottles of a very fine and rare Australian cognac) for a dog sled. Stinky still hasn't forgiven me. He says the charabanc held sentimental memories for him, although what they can be I can only guess. He won the thing in a poker game – but only after he'd lost his estate in Hampshire and the hunting lodge in the Trossachs to a smooth talking, white suited Texan in a back street bar on the outskirts of Houston. As I recall there was an ugly scene that night as a sobbing Stinky, after handing over the deeds and downing several shots of brandy and lime, accused the Texan of cheating, and as he lunged at the sneering fellow with what would have been a very impressive left hook, two aces and a king fell from the lace ruffles of Stinky's sleeve.

In the stunned silence that followed Stinky managed to leg it, vaulting through a window (which unfortunately was closed at the time) and limped out into the night. Luckily he'd had the presence of mind to grab up a set of keys as he went, and by dint of trying them in the locks of all the vehicles parked outside, had discovered that they belonged to a venerable VW camper van painted purple and liberally decorated with flora and yellow smiley faces. As it roared into life with a splutter and a bang after only the fourth attempt, Stinky, glancing into the rear view mirror, was gratified to see through the smoke the apparent owner of the charabanc holding back the mob. Evidently the thought of an insurance pay-out overcame the chap's indignation at having played cards with a very bad cheat.

But I digress, my old Cheese Flan. So here we are up in the Northern Territories where the aurora borealis nightly dances a smug little jig on the snowy horizon – a much over rated sight, I have to tell you. I've seen just as good displays lying in a warm gutter in Bangkok after a convivial evening drinking distilled rice stalks and chasing the dragon – and I didn't have to worry about my extremities freezing and dropping off as I watched them!

We didn't actually mean to come up here. I'd rather fancied the idea of a sojourn in Phuket myself, but since I was indisposed after an unfortunate mixing of clam chowder bought from a road side stand, and a dubious red wine harvested from a lesser known vineyard in South America and stored next to a radiator in Kalamazoo, I foolishly left the travel arrangements to Stinky. After he'd gallantly attempted to double our available funds by betting on an illegal mule race in Chicago, and lost, we found ourselves without the wherewithal for passage. That wouldn't have been too bad had not Stinky compounded the problem by referring to the jockey of his losing quadruped as the son of a badly wounded, inbred, mentally-challenged orphan whose right to breed should have been curtailed at birth. It then transpired that said father was none other than Luigi Polti, main hit man for the infamous Scar-Face Capone, great-nephew thrice removed of the great Al himself, owner of a string of dodgy kebab houses and head of one of the unofficially ruling Families of the city.

Needless to say we had to leg it out of Chicago with all the speed we could manage, and decided that heading in a northerly direction towards the Canadian border would give us our best chance of escape. There was a tense moment at the border when Stinky suddenly remembered that he was *persona non gratis* in Canada due to an unfortunate incident a couple of years ago with the ambassador's dog in a London park one dark, damp November night, compounded by another, even more unfortunate incident with the fellow's daughter. And son.

Fortunately a bit of rummaging in the old rucksack dragged out an alternative passport and with a quick nip to a drug store to obtain hair dye, fake tan and a pair of bottle-bottom glasses, we were able to get passed the guards with no more than the lightest of interrogation and probings.

Unfortunately it seems that Luigi Polti was a man of some determination, which rather surprised me in light of what I thought was a very minor sort of insult, in the scheme of things. It was as we sheltered from the hail of bullets under the ample skirt of an obliging can can dancer (who, to my consternation, turned out to be a drag artist) in a themed bar outside Winnipeg, that Stinky apologetically confided to me that not only had he insulted Polti through his son, but had also stolen his Cartier watch and gold cuff links with a very neat sleight of hand in a lingering after-apology handshake.

So, through the good offices of the can can dancer, who suffered the merest of flesh wounds as he sidled out of the door with us tucked away under his petticoats, we made our escape, headed farther north and took shelter in a rather seedy little brothel called, rather predictably, Eskimo Nell's in Saskatoon. It was while we were passing the time in that establishment, me practising my bar tending skills and Stinky choreographing the floor show (he has, I am rather uncomfortable about admitting, developed a real aptitude for seductively divesting himself of various articles of clothing, a skill that he is not shy in demonstrating with the littlest prompting – or indeed with no prompting at all – and which he is more than delighted to pass on to any willing pupils), that we met a wizened, squint-eyed, dentally challenged old fellow by the name of Yukon Pete. Yukon Pete had an amazing amount of wonga to slosh around considering that in apparel and smell he resembled nothing so much as an old stuffed bear that had been baked in the sun for a while, then left out in the rain for several months, rubbed back and forth through several small shrubs, dipped in a vat of whiskey and been used by the local dogs as a bathroom facility.

Being a sociable sort of fellow I did not let Pete's startling looks and odour deter me from accepting the drinks he so kindly pressed upon me, and indeed I even went so far as to suggest that a friendly game of poker might lighten the odd evening since a regrettable accident involving an ice pick, a tangled rope and a rather excitable sled dog rendered him incapable of enjoying any of the other delights Nell's could offer him. In the course of one such game, after the liquor had been flowing freely, Yukon Pete let slip that his ability to scatter largesse with such wanton abandon was due to the fact that he had in his possession a map that had been given to him many years ago by a dying Inuit who also happened to be blind. The poor fellow was under the misapprehension that he was passing the map on to his oldest son, a good friend of Pete's who had just stepped out of the hut for a moment. That map showed the way to a gold mine that the Inuit had been working diligently, and to no avail, for many years but which was now on the point of yielding an inordinate amount of profit. Yukon Pete, with a lamentable lack of consideration or loyalty to his friend, stuffed the map into his jacket, nipped smartly out of a small window to the side of the hut, cracked the whip gleefully over the heads of his waiting huskies, and sped off to collect provisions and head on up to the Yukon

Well, when I heard how Pete had come by the map I felt no compunction at all about relieving him of it as soon as he slumped forward into a puddle of beer on the table in front of him, although the memory of reaching into the fetid and crawling layers of his clothing will haunt me to my dying day.

And that is why, my old Fruit, I am sending you this card. It has been posted in the last outpost of civilisation before the North Pole, and just in case you don't see me again I wanted you to know that Stinky and I have at least died very rich men.

Must go now. I can see Stinky outside wrestling with the sled dogs. Didn't think dachshunds were any good in the snow, but the chap here assures me they're game little blighters and much more useful than they look, which can only be a good thing as the motley team he's just flogged us look about as useful as a trap door in a canoe. But you've got to trust the experts, haven't you?

Toodle pip, and love to all the offspring and those other relatives of mine who have emigrated down to the wilds of the West Country somewhere, Wotsername and Oojamaflip. Jolly brave chaps, is all I can say about them.

GUH.

Nic caught sight of one of the Great Uncle's missives and said he was my alter ego. What sort of an observation is that?

Jay said he was my hubris. It seems that Jessica has swallowed a dictionary and doesn't know what she's talking about.

And if Nic considers GUH to be my alter ego, what exactly does that mean he thinks about me?? Should I expect divorce proceedings to be instigated? – Should I be the one to instigate them??

Ann ignored GUH completely. I think she's the wisest.

"Greetings Uggling! (*yes, I get it. The weather is now too cold for an old boot, so it's time to bring out the Uggs. Ha ha – you're not going to out-weird me, Mowl!*)

I am very sure you have had forecasts of rain, storms, hail, gale-force winds, death, destruction and diarrhoea spreading from the 'West', mmmmmm? Well guess wot? We had it first – and in all it's glory! Now I have a conflict here. Whilst I would be the first to say that for it to rain in the night and be nice during the day is a Good Thing, I am also somewhat peeved (and bleary-eyed) when I have lain awake for hours as the rain lashed down, the wind howled, the hail danced a fandango and the thunder had a row with the farmer's dog (who shouted about it for the rest of the night) and the dustbin went walkies down the road with a clatter and a bang, and then wake up to a beautiful crisp, sunny, calm day which seems to say: 'Who? – Me?' to the basilisk glare rolled upon it from under a very wild and tousled heap of velvet. The dawn may well have blushed!

And then, guess wot? Come night time, up comes Brer Wind along with his mates rain, hail, dawg, etcetera, to keep up the good times for us for another night of earplugs, head under the pillow and general grogginess the next morning.

Over to you. Enjoy!

No doubt you will get the left-over gentle breezes and little shower of rain just to green up your sun-parched garden. I am counting my blessings. And counting how long between the thunder and the lightening to see if I have to shiver off into the study to unplug the computer and then shiver off down to the lounge to unplug the telly. Or send Lam shivering down to do it for us. The good thing about Lam's is that they don't stop for thinking and conflabs. They just go. Whoosh! – all unplugged and cold feet back on warm back. Hey ho.

Today's weather forecast mentions localised flooding in the south-west. That sounds like fun. The last time we had localised flooding (last week, as I recall) it caused me some fun and games.

Things You Need To Know About Mowls (for the sake of the following story, anyway):

1. Lam

2. Specs

3. Small battered car

4. Hair straighteners

5. Quivers

6. Likes making a splash

7. Localised flooding expected in south-west means:

8. Rain on specs

9. Steam on said specs when added to warm snout and small battered car.

As well as localised flooding we also had many road works, changed priorities and new road layouts. So:

Rain + dark + street lighting + steam and rain on specs = can't quite see the new road markings, which means: one Mowl sailing down nice new empty lane (newly made over for buses only, but hey, a little red paint here and there ......) to the accompaniment of horns, shouts and waved fists. Probably. Vision clouded by steam on specs means that I could not be sure on this point. But I did see that nice man gesturing to me that there are now TWO lanes.

Another thing about Cornwall is the hills. Or, more to the point, the valleys between the hills. Where the rain collects. So now we have: rain + winter (ie: soggy fallen leaves + drains) = large puddles, which in turn means: One Mowl in small battered car whooshing down the water slide straight into what I took to be the Tamar but which was in fact Budshead Road to the accompaniment of much splashing, engine choking and a piercing mew!

State of one Mowl come evening: damp + steaming + quivering + curly.

Lam, meanwhile, had a job in St Germans (only the Cornish could have canonised the Germans for attacking the English. I'm still trying to work out St Erney. Sounds like a London saint to me, like a St Fred) which means he had to negotiate the Cornish country roads – you just know where this is heading; into a ditch, you're thinking. Well, not quite. It was a puddle that had aspirations to becoming a lake and was practising in a little lane where it thought it would be undisturbed. Lam did face down the puddle like a Man, and valiantly drove through. Age is showing though – he did it slowly and cautiously. Good thing too, he said that when it reached the bonnet he decided to back up (makes him sound like a drain, doesn't it? – Ah, memories of Cyprus!) and go the long miles round the other way with sharks still gripped to his exhaust pipe!

Aren't you going to visit us soon? How can you ignore the temptation? You can surf down on an alpaca.

I bet my garden's greener than yours. I just know my patio is!!

We had a note through the door from the local council. They are trying to re-market Saltash and the surrounding areas. They have set up a special 'think tank' and named it Saltash Creative Re-planning And Progression Plan (SCRAPP). I will let you know some of the juicy bits. I think a park-and-ride for Plymouth was mentioned. Odd, you may say, becoming a car park for they foreigners up the line, but only think for a mo! – *They pay on this side of the river!* Ha ha! We get they money an' good riddance to they foreigners! – 'Xept it may be good Cornish folk goin' over to that there rat-infested den of iniquity. Probably not. Just they foreigners like us wot 'as moved in an teken all they houses an' jobs an' encourages their families to come down with they caravans across That Bridge.

They have also outlined several other (expensive) projects which I doan 'old with. And they want a logo.

How about a pasty rampant on a field of yawn? Sounds like a winner, huh?

The trouble is I'm not sure what Saltash is actually known for. (Stop it!) We used to have a cockle pickle alley, and we have an annual King Cockle event, so maybe some kind of cockle logo. I may regret this, but just what does a cockle look like? Surely there is more to it than that grey and orange gritty mess you get on a very small plate and cover with pepper and vinegar?

I am sure that Great Things are afoot and shall keep you informed.

Love twall
Mowl

PS: We nearly had a ceremonial flushing of the linseed down the loo this weekend. I caught a cold. I have suffered and gone without all these weeks and had just bragged that, although two members of our office had had colds, I, the Big Sneeze, had not. And then wot happens? The old snout lets me down big time! I got chucked out of work on Wednesday lunchtime (I should not really have gone in but it was month end, short staff, etc, etc, moan, grumble, martyr) and retired to bed alternately sneezing, shivering, and sweating and very, very grumpy. I could have cried. Still, on calmer note I thought 'Rome (or my resistance) wasn't built in a day (or even a few weeks)' so I (sort of) decided to stick with it. I did rebel and had some chips with my steak and salad and some slightly illegal junk – crisps, etc – when we dragged people over to watch a film the other evening. Well, you have to give them something more than a pound of brussel sprouts, and you have to be sociable. I keep quiet about the very illegal glass of red wine. So, hand down the loo to retrieve the old linseed oil and back to the rabbit food. And the steamer.

And to add insult to injury (or perhaps injury to insult in this case) I broke a tooth on a healthy, nutritious seed! I maintain that I never broke a tooth on a cream bun yet! – So much for this healthy eating lark. I also got one (a linseed would you believe!) stuck up under my gum.

I have to admit, however, that the cold did not last as long as usual and was certainly a lot drier (let's leave it at that, shall we?) than usual, so maybe it's working ...... Bah, no excuse for a real binge now!

Bye again.
Mowl (with a tissue (atishoo??) and attitude)"

Poor Mowl.

Chapter Twenty-One

We are having our staircase moved. I don't really know why. It has served every inhabitant of this cottage well in its present situation (in a cupboard in the kitchen) for a hundred and forty-three years. But Nic had been busy with his drawing board and said that if we moved it we could have more room in the kitchen, which we could definitely do with, and that it would look lovely in the living room, which is plenty big enough to accommodate it, if we had a nice ornate oak balustrade.

So the testosterone level in the house has risen considerably as builders have moved in for a while. There is a lot of coughing and shouting and banging and whistling and bustling and the pulling up of trousers to cover the traditional "builder's smile". Reeb is now afraid to go outside – not that our chaps are disrespectful or anything, but they do tend to watch her and do a bit of strutting and like to engage her in friendly banter, which the Little Reeb finds disconcerting.

Ann has been very interested in the goings on up here. She even had a few not very helpful suggestions about how we could access our bedrooms and (more importantly) the loo in the brief period when the old staircase was removed and the new one fit to be used. No matter that I assured her this would not happen, her imagination had been fired and the suggestions came thick and fast. Many of them involving Kester's Diabolical Machine. I made the mistake of showing them to Kester, and I did not like the look of the light that came into his eye.

It would have been nice to get away from the mess for a while, but really one needs to be on hand when workmen are dismantling your house or you could come back to some nasty surprises. Ann and Chris, having no such problems, did take a quick break away from winter to the kindlier climes of Spain for a few days.

It comes to something when your hens receive a postcard from your sister and you don't. Oh sure, two cards were sent from sun-soaked Spain (rub it in, why doesn't she), but the one not addressed to Duracell, EverReady and Nicad (Attila the Hen, by the way, is still smarting from the insult of exclusion. We are consoling one another), the one containing a rather rude little ditty involving thorns and bums, was addressed to All Residents, etc. I can only assume that I fall within the "etc" category. Perhaps it's revenge for the Ole Dime a Dozen epithet placed upon a small, round child once in the dim and distant past. Anyway, I now know my place. I shall sit quietly in my little gloomy corner. Just call me Eeyore and pass me a thistle to munch on.

We still seem to be getting the West Country's weather, and we don't want it. I thought the deal was that they wrung out the clouds before sending them along. Well I can tell you that it's not working! Yesterday afternoon I saw all four hens crammed into a trug which whirled away down the drive like a little coracle, spinning gently as it went, and if it hadn't been for the log-jam of alpacas in the gateway I'm sure they would have been washed into the ditch, rushed passed Squallory's dam and away to the distant horizon.

The Owl is thinking of turning the Diabolical Machine into an ocean going vessel now that, reluctantly, he admits that with the installation of stairs indoors there will be no need for Ann's "kindly" suggestion of a form of propulsion for catapulting mothers into upper storey windows of the house. He clung to that idea for quite some time, suggesting that it could always be on stand-by for emergencies. I told him (a little tartly, I will admit) that I could foresee no emergency EVER for the use of such a thing, but I could see that the hope lingered.

And after the rain – snow! Not as much as in London, apparently, but still a nice little smattering which (to Small's delight) meant that her school was closed today. Nic phone me – once I was safely at work – to say that he was going to take Small sledging. Darn. I would give a lot to see Nic hurtling down a steep slope on a tea-tray, his grey hair streaming out behind him. I would give even more to see him pitch into a snow drift at the end of the hurtle. But apparently that was not to be. I was at Work. Poo.

Acted in true Good Wife way next morning by stopping off during the blizzard at Waitrose in order to stock up on provisions in case of a Big Freeze. We're always frightened of a Big Freeze here in England, aren't we? The fact that, despite the buglings of the media and dire forecasts almost every year that This Is It – this is going to be the Worst Winter EVER – it never actually happens does not allay these fears one jot, and before the first snowflake has managed to settle we have to rush to the supermarket to buy industrial quantities of tea, sugar, long-life milk, biscuits, toilet rolls and candles. These are the stock items, obligatory to have by in case of the Big Freeze, the Big Strike or indeed the Big Drought. So long as we British have our steaming mugs of tea (brewed over the candles if necessary), a digestive biscuit to dunk into it, and are secure in the knowledge that our bowels are well taken care of, we can face anything. Bring it on.

Having said that, I like the snow. I like the snow, that is, in this day and age when we can retreat to a lovely, warm house once we've tobogganed down a few hills, hurled snowballs at one another, rescued husbands or children from ditches (or not) and got thoroughly wet and cold.

Our hens are not so keen, however, and I see it as yet another excuse for them not to lay any eggs. The excuses are getting many and varied, and quite frankly I'm getting a little fed up with them. Apparently there is no excuse at all for me to neglect piling a little more fresh hay into their nest boxes, or braving the elements to load up their feeding troughs, but that's hens for you.

The alpacas too seem to like the white weather. Looked out this morning and saw them standing in the blizzard, a tear in their eyes as they thought wistfully of their ancestral home, the Andes. Monty was playing mournfully on the pan pipes and Dylan was scanning the skies hopefully (or perhaps fearfully, you never can tell with an alpaca) for sight of a condor cruising majestically up above. Mind you I have my suspicions that all this nostalgia and the brave front shown by them standing in the worst of the blizzard for a few minutes (when they knew I'd be making the tea and therefore looking out of the window) is just a show. I rather think that in actual fact they have become somewhat acclimatised to our more temperate British weather because a little later on I got a grubby note pushed under the door. It was scrawled on an old Tesco receipt (which had obviously been caught in the hedge at some time) and covered in muddy hoof prints. It said, in very scrawled writing (and a little tersely, I thought), that I'd taken six bags of wool from them over the years, and where were the scarves and mittens they had been promised? I remember no such promise, but that's alpacas for you.

If this snow continues I think I shall have to train Arfer to pull a sledge for when the provisions run low and I have to forage for more. Mind you, I have a horrible suspicion that there will be a short scuffle and I shall find myself in the harness and Arfer up behind with a whip! And that's dogs for you.

Luckily the weather had not affected our internet connection, so I settled down to see what I'd got.

"Greetings Flea Bag!" (*Wot??!*)
"So you've got snow, have you? We too have snow. We

have the Really Big Freeze. We have been brought to a standstill!

You may have seen it on the weather maps as a tiny white glimmer that flickered over Plymouth and was gone. We have an inch. And we have mayhem!

Just for a moment – one sparkling, blissful moment – wouldn't I love to transfer the average Janner (Plymouthian to you uninitiated foreigners) to Yorkshire. Or Scotland. Or Canada. Sigh. Why can't they work out that it is just fluffy rain? Then they could sink back into their comfort zone and reach for another pasty instead of fretting and rushing about and bringing everything to a standstill.

Yesterday we were sent home from work. No, not because of the weather. We had no snow yesterday. But we did have a burst water main outside the factory and, with up to six hundred staff, no canteen, no loos and (worst of all) no tea facilities, we got the order of the boot.

So being home with time on my hands, I decided to go through all the junk mail that had been accumulating and dispose of that which we can do without.

Don't you just love those catalogues you get with all of those wonderful little gadgets that you apparently can't live without? We had several, so I sat down with a warming something and browsed. They lift the very soul and I immediately felt an e-mail coming on (a bit like a bowel movement. Sweeps upon you when you least expect it, and is very satisfying when it's over).

Don't get me wrong, some of the things are really useful – like the Unisex Mac in a Sac, Dog Rocks, Tattoo Sleeves and Welly Warmers, and I really *do* like the floral clogs and floral garden tools. But how, O how, did I ever live without the Onion Goggles? For a mere £14.99 you can purchase these items, tastefully produced in lime green and white with 'a comfortable foam seal around the goggles to ensure a perfect fit to protect your eyes from onion vapours'. Answer the door to the milkman sporting those nifty little numbers and you may not have to wait for the dog to see him off!

And O! – How I wish that I had seen the Musical Cake Slice in time for your wedding! £8.99 'Celebrate in style with this amusing musical cake slice. You and your guests can sing along to the Wedding March or For He's a Jolly Good Fellow'. Imagine the bride's face! – Imagine the groom's face as it is bourn upon him that this woman with the cake slice is now family and cannot be ignored!

There were many mentions of items 'for your Aga' which did make me wonder if, in fact, the catalogue was aimed at a higher demographic (reminiscent of the gardening book I once read which exhorted with the immortal words: 'No matter how small your garden, plant at least a quarter of an acre of woodland') and that a chortling pleb like me did not understand the vital necessity of owning mango splitters, USB Coffee Warmers ('Simply plug into the USB port of your computer, place your drink on the hot plate and it will keep warm. PC Mac and laptop compatible'), Magnetic Wristbands, Sonic Scrubbers and Gloves in a Bottle. But when I came across a Paint Your Own Gnome kit and was reassured that when I placed the finished article, resplendent in glow-in-the-dark waistcoat and hat, out on my front lawn I would be the envy of my neighbours, I almost succumbed to temptation.

There was an excellent Aero Garden – 'Grow herbs, tomatoes or salad all year round – no green fingers needed! This idiot-proof gadget uses NASA-tested aeroponic technology to grow plants faster, more reliably, with no soil, weeds or mess.' Idiot proof. Hmmmm. Is this the same company that pronounced a radio controlled plane 'Unbreakable' and, following an impassioned call from a distraught Lam relabelled it 'Virtually unbreakable'? But at a mere £129.99 for the garden, £14.99 per kit (herbs, toms, salad, etc), another £14.99 for two replacement grow bulbs (recommended after six months) the whole thing should become cost-effective after about seventy-five years or so! And aren't NASA the ones who spent thousands of tax payers dollars producing a pen that would write in zero gravity while the Russians used a pencil?

The Bug Zappa ('Swat the fly with this battery operated Bug Zappa and as soon as it touches the mesh it will be electrocuted. This could go down in history as a new sport and it's a great way to practise tennis!') offers many possibilities which I'm sure the manufacturer did not foresee. One can see the glee in the average husband's eye as he contemplates swatting a wife's bot with it! – Imagine that being cited in court as grounds for divorce! – And could the husband sue the Bug Zappa company for damages following that divorce?

I was seriously tempted by the 'Computing for the Older Generation'. 'These guides, written especially for the over 50's, use plain English and avoid technical jargon. Produced in large, clear type, they are easy to read'. I said LARGE, CLEAR TYPE, dear. Have you got your hearing aid switched on? Shall I send you the catalogue so that you can purchase one of these books?

My favourites, however, had to be the unisex Happy-Pee and Uriwell. 'Do you dread being "caught short" in a traffic jam, or miles from a loo? Keep one of these reusable Uriwells in your glovebox or handbag (?) and never worry again. The size of a Coke can, the device can be used by men, women and children and expands when necessary'. Wouldn't you just *love* for a mugger to take that handbag?

For just us girls there is the Shewee. 'If you have ever envied a man's ability to "go" almost anywhere, now you can too! This clever device allows women to pee without removing clothes. No more bare bottoms or difficulty balancing over squat loos. Reusable and machine washable. Now also available in pink'.

I am so glad it is now available in pink. I might have some serious doubts about my femininity after being, at last, able to pee like a man! There is a picture (not a photograph) demonstrating this handy little item being used, and it has a specially designed rigid storage case, perfect for holding a

Shewee together with an extension pipe 7 ½ x 2 ½ x 1 ½ . A mere £6.99 for the Shewee, £1.99 for the extension pipe and £3.99 for the storage case. This is labelled as a best seller.

Also for us girls are the Silicone Nipple Covers – 'End embarrassment when wearing a T-shirt on chilly days'. (Personally I'm all for a thick thermal vest!) This is another best seller.

O for a Bathroom Squid! This is something that sticks to the wall using numerous suction pads, and then you stick your shampoo, shower gel – and probably your Shewee as well – to the suction pads on the other side.

Imagine! – There is a flying alarm clock! 'Do you know someone who has trouble getting up in the morning? When the alarm rings the propeller launches into the air and flies around the room. The only way to turn off the alarm is to get up, locate the disc and return it to its base! A brilliant present for teenagers!' Justifiable homicide comes to mind.

I was seriously tempted by the Pretty Useful Tools – floral hammer, screwdriver and pliers – Lam is always nicking mine, imagine him turning up to a building site with the floral hammer – yes!!

The Fresh Drop Smell Stop seemed rather boring until I noticed that it was delicately advertised as 'Combating those nasty niffs that can cause embarrassment after a visit to the loo. Best used prior to the "event" for maximum benefit'. Sigh.

There was a high quality porcelain 'I'm Cooking' reminder magnet. For blondes. Talking of which, I know a blond – male, resident of Cranbrook Drive but who shall remain nameless – who put a small potato in the microwave oven for ten minutes and forgot to look at his 'I'm Cooking' reminder magnet and was reminded only by the clarion call of the smoke alarm. We did not quite have flames but even now, three days later, the house is still redolent of eau-de-singed-spud! We should have used the Fresh Drop, but maybe it would not have been effective after the "event"!

So along with the reminder magnet, I was thinking of ordering him a very timely and useful 'Dinner Will Be Ready When You Hear the Smoke Alarm' pinny!

I had a wonderful afternoon. I wonder when the next catalogue will drop tantalisingly onto the doormat?

Yours, intrigued

Mowl"

I think I've received one of those catalogues. Or twelve.

Mind you, I firmly believe that Ann's e-mail is proof positive that there are such things as guardian angels - mine was definitely working overtime around my wedding. The musical cake slice must have had him/her preparing a few lightening bolts (I know, angels are supposed to be kind, holy creatures, but one must also remember the cherubs guarding the way back to Eden with a fiery sword, so I am convinced that my GA would have a quiver full of lightening bolts to protect me from the machinations - er, sorry, kindly thoughts and intentions, of my Wicked Kid Sis) to aim in her direction had she been overwhelmed by this unseemly desire. And I'm sure that the musical cake slice would have been the least of my problems. Despite my entreaty for "no presents" I can only guess at what delightful packages Nic and I would have received upon that auspicious day - all neatly wrapped (probably in sparkly paper and with and abundance of pom-poms and tassels) and with a gleeful Mowl exhorting us to open them at the reception in order to share the joy with the other guests. The joy, of course, would have been entirely the Mowl's; but that's another matter.

Back to the catalogues. I must admit to owning several of the items which Ann so mercilessly derided. Quite frankly I don't know where I'd be without my wellie warmers, the dog rocks (to prevent dog wee from killing the lawn. Arfer keeps trying to lift them out of his water bowl, but I firmly replace them) and floral tool kit (purchased for exactly the reason Ann contemplated them. It keeps the Owl at bay). And I must admit to have toyed (is that the right word??) with the

Shewee. Had I known it came in pink I would have sent off for it immediately. (Does this last item at last prove Freud correct? - Do we women really all suffer from penis envy?? I didn't know I did until now. Especially as it can be pink and fitted with an extension pipe, although one cannot help but wonder why. What do you need it longer for??? - If I was going to "wee like a man" I would want to get as close as possible to whatever it was I was wee-ing on (one presumes a tree or wall??), not stand about four feet away and aim ..... although .....)

The catalogue was still on my mind when I went to work the next day. About mid morning after my third cup of tea of the day, I went and looked enviously at the Gents loos, then skulked off to the inferior Ladies.

There was an e-mail from Rugg. I was expecting it – although not on the office computer. He had told me over the phone that he was writing to a hotel in Eastbourne where he and Marie had stayed for a weekend recently. Rugg had fallen over a glass table which some bright spark had thought a good idea to put in a dimly lit area of the hotel's library, and severely damaged his leg.

He was annoyed by the fact that the hotel management will not accept liability for his injury, but blame him for the fall. He has contacted injury lawyers, but they say there is but a slim chance of him getting a favourable hearing at court. He has written direct to the hotel, but been brushed aside with a trite little letter which thanked him for his feedback and hoped they could look forward to his patronage in the future. And all this is riling him even more.

Anyway, I listened to his grievances and offered what little advice I could, and then he said that he was at last giving up on the matter but wanted to send a final, very sarcastic "feedback" letter to the hotel saying how he felt about their attitude towards his mishap, and enclosing photographs of his leg. However, he wanted to run his letter by me first to get my opinion of it and make sure it had the right "tone". A wise move since Rugg's sarcasm is so dry as to be positively Saharan and very often goes way over people's heads.

So here was the e-mail from Rugg telling me that he was attaching the letter we had talked about. Indeed I saw the attachment. In fact there were three. One was titled "letter.jpg", the next "ani_gif" and the third "Ashley.wps".

I tried to open the first. It would not open.

I fiddled about and finally it did open, to reveal a very pretty picture of dolphins.

I closed it.

I opened the second one. It too was exactly the same pretty picture of dolphins.

Suspecting I already knew what I was going to find, I opened the third and, yes, there was another picture of dolphins.

I thought it must be me, that I was doing something wrong, so I went back and tried to open them all again. Still dolphins. Called Richard and asked if he could do anything with the attachments, but he couldn't. Telephoned Reeb at home to ask for advice and she made a few suggestions, but they didn't work. We still got dolphins. Tried printing the files without opening them, and now have three very lovely pictures of dolphins, which I'm sure Small will love to have.

Knowing Rugg was awaiting my response, I phoned him.

"Dad," I said, "I got your e-mail, but I can't seem to open the files."

There was that growly groan Rugg does when he knows he's done something Ruggish and is now going to have to explain himself.

"I know," he said. "They're gone."

"What do you mean, gone?"

"Lost, gone, swallowed up into the ether," he clarified.

"But there are three files attached to your e-mail," I said, "although they all show pictures of dolphins."

"Yes," said Rugg in exasperation, "and I can't seem to get rid of the blasted things."

Didn't really know how to respond to this. Perhaps I should contact Ann and let her know that Rugg is apparently afflicted with a plague of dolphins and may possibly need help. I feel I've done my bit.

Chapter Twenty-Two

Jay has acquired a new dog, and Kester has left home.

These two events are in no way linked, except that they both affect me. I will dwell awhile upon the new dog. Kester's departure has taken up rather more of my contemplation than I would like, so I shall wrench my thoughts away from him and talk about the dog.

Jay and Darren have mentioned quite a few times that they would rather like a dog. Jay has always had a penchant for a whippet. A nice little friendly whippet. Small, cute and faithful. Short-haired, delicately proportioned and quiet. A pocket-sized dog, if you will, to be a companion and source of delight, a friend to accompany her on her walks and drives, small and unobtrusive and gently trembling.

Darren, on the other hand, likes Big. One of his customers eulogised about his dog, a black Russian terrier, which was a relatively new breed, big and exotically long-haired. Darren was intrigued. A few months later that same customer remarked that a friend of his had a year old black Russian terrier dog that needed re-homing. They were expensive dogs, but this couple were desperate and would give the dog away to a good home. Darren was hooked. Jay, peering over his shoulder as he researched this fascinating new breed on the internet remarked, a little nervously, that they looked awfully large. Darren said, airily, that they weren't *that* big. Not as big as a great Dane or an Irish wolfhound, for instance. Jay agreed, but remarked that they did look as big as Newfoundlands, and in her books that was Big.

The long and the short of it was that Darren brought the dog, Moscow, home assuring Jay that it was just for a meeting, no strings attached and with no obligation. Of course as soon as the big, hairy, lolloping Moscow bounced into the house, wiping the low coffee table clear of all objects with one sweep of his long, curly tail, and slobbering Darren with wet canine kisses, Jay knew she was beaten. Food bowls, a favourite squeaky toy and a lead were pressed into Jay's weak hands as Darren wrestled with his new friend on the floor, and the erstwhile owners of Moscow nearly tripped over themselves in their haste to get down the drive and into their car.

Not that there is anything wrong with Moscow, exactly, except that he is not just big, but inordinately clumsy with it. If he turns too quickly on the wooden floors of Jay and Darren's house, he falls over. If you frighten him, by which I merely mean, come into a room when he's not expecting it, which is often since he can't see much of anything with the fringe of black curls that hangs over his eyes, he falls over. He collides with things. He goes through things rather than round them, be they hedges, dustbins or small children. Moscow, with his big flat feet and straight back, has a decidedly peculiar look about him – he looks like a man in a dog suit rather than a real dog. The fact that he is extremely loving and friendly could be said to be a redeeming feature, except when he slobbers you with his wet chops, or tries to climb onto your lap when you sit down.

Anyway, Moscow is now firmly ensconced in the Jay/Darren residence and very much a part of the family. Such is Darren's love for the big, cuddly creature that even the unfortunate events of last week have been forgiven by him, although Jay is still in need of a soothing word when she recalls the incident.

Jay was upstairs in their house when she heard a peculiar noise. She listened for a moment and thought that a neighbour was jet washing their car, or perhaps their driveway. She peered out of the bedroom window to see who it was. There was no such activity going on, and yet the noise continued. Jay stood and listened again. Funny, she thought, it sounds like it's coming from inside the house. Curious, she went down the stairs to investigate, only to find, to her utter horror that the noise was that made by a very large, incontinent black Russian terrier coating the entire downstairs floor with the contents of his bowels.

Jay was practically in tears when she told me this sorry tale. I clucked and soothed, but was secretly glad that someone else was having animal problems, and it wasn't just me. Does that make me a bad mother? Oh dear.

And so, as I said above, Kester has left home. It seems unbelievable. To my maternal way of thinking he is still in nappies and totally dependent upon me to feed and clothe him, and I was convinced that within a month of leaving my tender care he would be lying dead in miserable squalor and degradation, killed by hyperthermia, food poisoning or malnutrition. But the fact is (much as I can't or won't admit it) he is a grown man (just) and has moved in with his fiancée, Michelle.

Now when a young man leaves home he usually does one of two things: either he embarks upon a period of raucous, alcohol fuelled wild-oat sowing, or, if a girl friend is involved, he settles down to staid suburban maturity, much to the marvel of his parents and hooting disbelief of his siblings.

Trust Kester to find a third way.

The accommodation Kester and Michelle have found comes with a garage. A large garage. Personally I fully believe that it was the lure of the Large Garage that took Kester from the bosom of his family rather than Love alone. I say this because in the days leading up to his departure there was a lot of excited talk about the dimensions of this garage, sketches of conversion plans with sound-proofing, false ceilings, inspection pits and (ambitiously) basements with what looked suspiciously like tunnels leading from them.

Catalogues from tool companies began arriving thick and fast, and Nic was earnestly questioned about what weight the company Transit could carry. Curtains, rugs, cutlery and bed linen featured not at all.

And so the Owlmaster flew the nest, and I shed a tear.

The Diabolical Machine went with him.

That should have been a relief. However, Reeb, watching the Thing being loaded onto the back of the Transit along with Kester's two computers, punch bag, kendo suit, survival books and underwater harpoon (don't ask. I never did) pondered, aloud, what he was going to do with it now he and it were leaving what she (laughingly) called my parental control. She then, quite callously, I thought, proceeded to list a number of increasingly hair raising options she thought could well be possibilities.

It got me thinking. And shuddering.

Sigh.

That says it all.

It is a motherly sigh heaved after being reminded of Things Her Son Has/Will/Might Do/Done and which she has managed to shove, kicking and screaming and trying to claw its way back out, to the dark recesses of her mind with the aid of several large G&Ts and a small mallet (applied by a far-too willing child to the back of her head). A large door then being firmly shut upon said thoughts and heavy chains padlocked across it, a notice, writ large (possibly in blood) would be placed upon the metal studded boards warning the conscious mind not ever, even in a wild and bored moment, to peer behind that door.

So the DM has left our premises. There is no jubilation in this statement. Only Fear. The Owlmaster blasting himself to Kingdom Come (or perhaps a mere orbit of Earth) from whatever starting point is something that makes me tremble and sometimes even gibber quietly to myself. Apparently I am not alone. Once the move was complete and Michelle had moved in I asked Kester what she thought of the Advent of the Beast. He said that Michelle, after a few polite enquiries as to what he's up to when he shuffles off to his workshop (generally clad (worryingly) in flameproof overalls, toetector boots and a face mask, with eyebrows suitably Vaselined against assault), has now told him point blank and very firmly not to tell her what he gets up to when he goes to the garage, ever. She is wiser than she looks. (Apparently (by the way) she has categorically banned Kester from installing a settee or indeed anything resembling a comfy chair, a kettle or a Play Station in the garage. She knows that should that happen, she will never, ever see him. See - a wise woman).

And it gets worse. I had an excited Kester call round last Friday asking if I thought Bob and Mike from work would be willing to help him with a Project (just as an aside, it will be noticed that the Lam's good offices were not suggested to be sought. This is because I Put My Foot Down on that score (knowing a Lam as I do) and some time ago stated with all the vehemence I could muster, reinforced with a basilisk glare, that Kester was on no account to pick Lam's brains about anything Diabolically Mechanical as it could well lead to and Irreconcilable Rift within the Family). Anyway, to continue, my tongue then asked - before Brain, who had been momentarily distracted by the sight of Kester's face in Joy mode and was trying to compute this anomaly, could stop it - what the project was.

I knew I didn't want to know. I knew that I, as Mother, couldn't handle the answer. But the question was out, and no matter that I chewed my tongue to a bloody stump in punishment, Kester was ready, dewy eyed and breathless, to divulge. Apparently he has been offered by someone (and believe me, I shall find out their name and hunt them down like a dog) a rather ancient Rolls Royce aeronautical engine for a mere couple of hundred quid. This engine, so I am reliably informed by an ecstatic Owl, may be small, but it has a considerable amount of thrust, enough, in fact, to propel a Boy, suitably strapped into a home made Harrier Jump Jet type aircraft, upwards at a very decent velocity. It might then even go forwards and perhaps perform a few aerial stunts to the awe and amazement of an appreciative crowd of his friends and well-wishers.

Or it might then hurtle groundwards, crash and burst into flames (I pointed out, a little hysterically, through the bloody bubbles foaming around my mouth) - but Kester was airily dismissive of this possibility.

Any faint and foolish hopes I may have entertained about Bob and Mike being older and wiser and therefore ready to exert a Steadying Influence upon an eager Owl were dashed when Kester bowled up to our factory to tell them about the Project. I have a strong suspicion that the encouragement and enthusiasm they both displayed were in fact a way of getting at me. I'm not entirely sure why, indeed I may be mistaken on this point and allowing myself to become victim to unreasonable paranoia, I mean, what have I ever done to them? That is what Reason told me. But did I really imagine the gleeful looks cast my way by the two elderly gentlemen, the chortlings into sleeves and sniggers behind my back??? Actually, a form of personal "pay back" need not come into it at all; naturally all men are Little Boys at heart, and Getting One Over on a woman, especially a Mother, is gleeful to them any time.

So it looks like the Project is on. I'm already getting nostalgic about the DM which no doubt will be cast aside when the new girl comes to town.

Unbelievably (to me anyway) Kester and Michelle settled into domestic bliss with ease. There was a little difficulty involving a neighbour and parking rights – or rather, perceived rights – which threatened to get out of hand, but fortunately didn't. Other than that, life for the Owlmaster is looking good.

Ann has been following the Flight of the Owl with interest and I was not surprised to receive an e-mail on the subject.

"Wot Ho to the Floral Gumboot
(What a lovely word - Gumboot! You can really get the

old chops around Gumboot!)" (*Indeed, I would rather like to help her on that score ......*)

"I have not heard much about the Owlmaster and his bullying neighbour recently and I have A Theory. (General clearing of throat, shuffling of papers and mounting to the lectern.)

The Owlmaster is not quite the meek and victimised creature that his mother thinks (or dreams) him to be. He is an Owlmaster. And this is what has happened.

Being Decidedly Cunning, he has awaited the moment when the man of the house has gone off to work, or golf or preferably somewhere out of range of his mobile phone (spoken like a true Cornwall-girl (notice I did not dare to claim to be a Cor*nish* girl - 'not until your grandmother is in the graveyard!!' and I am not prepared to go and dig her up!) you probably don't have any 'out of mobile phone range' areas in Bedfordshire. We have a couple - Cornwall, Devon ....) and the wife is alone, happily flitting around with the duster.

Then the Owlmaster wheels out the Diabolical Machine.

Now, if she is, say, the average housewife and not of The Initiated (like his old Mum) she will not have a clue as to what this strange contraption is. She will peep out with increased nervousness and much twitching of the curtains as Kester nonchalantly oils, adjusts and improvises. She will run from room to room to get a better and more startling view. All she will comprehend is: protective wear, flames and The Mark of the Beast!

Then she will hit the sherry until her husband comes home.

By this time, of course, the DM will have been wheeled back into the garage. Out of sight.

When her husband eventually returns from intimidating his golfing partners into proclaiming his victory, the Thing (according to his wife, prostrate on the sofa, limp hand on pale forehead and gesturing with her sherry glass) will have grown tentacles, dripping fangs and become the size of the

Empire State Building having mown down twelve residents, eaten five children, two rottweilers and a squirrel!

Now, the husband will probably not quite believe this description, but he will know that there is - Something. The clue will be the subterranean rumblings as he approaches the boundary of the house. The scorch-marks around the garage door (marking the place where the Thing claws it's way out of the bowels of Hell to feed). And the fact that no birds sing over the house. Not an ounce of seagull guano in sight (sorry, Cornwall inserting itself again - that should read pigeon poo!). Just an eerie gathering of owls. Watching.

And then there is Kester. Unscathed. Except for his eyebrows. Which are missing. He is watching as one assessing possibilities: how far will this one make it up the road before he is dragged screaming into The Lair, his fingernails ploughing furrows along the Tarmac?

But the neighbour is an Englishman and, gripping his newspaper firmly with both hands he nods: 'Good evening', and retreats, stiff backed and with set jaw in good order to a stiff whisky and soda. He is followed by the Owlmaster's dark and brooding gaze.

Somewhere in the distance an owl hoots.

Now you are going to go and spoil it all by telling me that the DM is still in your barn and that Kester is silent because he has moved into his own garden shed with a white flag fluttering forlornly above it, and the neighbour has insinuated his distant relatives into Kester's house 'for a short stay of eleven years or so' and is spreading his empire up the street!

Do keep me up to date on Happenings.

Love Twall!!

M"

I do not appreciate the glee with which Others contemplate and discuss my son's exploits. There is no humour there for me. Only a sinking heart and a desire to throttle Certain People who blithely, indeed glibly, chirrup away about possible scenarios that had, without me knowing it, been formulating in my own mind but which I would not allow house room.

Perhaps I should go and visit Michelle and we can discuss him, shudderingly and in hushed whispers, over a glass or two of something reviving.

Chapter Twenty-Three

Small and I took a trip to north Wales to see Rugg and Marie, and we decided to take Arfer with us. Rugg's leg has not improved since his run in with the hotel glass coffee table, in fact it seems to be worsening, which is worrying. He is currently housebound and in some pain, and Marie is frazzled from looking after him and the house.

I borrowed Jay's satnav for the journey. There was absolutely no good reason for me to do so, I have to admit, since I've done the journey so often over the years, but it is a Novelty and as such must be tried out. I also reasoned that if I try it on a journey that I know very well I can judge its performance and therefore trust it (or not) on journeys into the Unknown (possibly at some time when I need to rescue Great Uncle Horatius from some dire situation ...... Hmmm. Is he beginning to cross the boundary between imagination and reality in my thinking? Should I be worried??))

Unfortunately, on the journey, I made an awful discovery about myself. Perhaps it will not be a discovery or surprise to anyone else. Perhaps they will say: Yes, so? – as indeed my own dear children did.

The discovery is that I have a quite monumental problem with authority, and a machine telling me, however kindly and for my own good, to turn left at a certain point makes me instinctively turn right. Small gave me a very worried look as I argued with Madge (as I had named the satnav lady) when she directed me one way and I *knew* it would be better if I went another, and then gloated shamelessly when I went my way and the "Miles to go" figure changed to less than it had originally been. We had a lot of "Do a U turn as soon as it is safe to do so" and "Recalculating ......" as I took a route different from the one she suggested.

Eventually arrived at Rugg and Marie's feeling rather satisfied with myself. Me: 1. Technology: 0.

This was the first time Arfer had ever been to Rugg and Marie's house and for some reason he took fright as he leaped out of the car and saw the two of them standing on the doorstep waiting to greet us. He faltered, his tail dropped, and then he bolted off down the road. I chased off after him and brought him back, but had quite a job persuading him to go into the house.

"It must be our new carpet that spooked him," Marie suggested.

I thought that a strange thing to say. If you lay a new carpet in your hallway and suspect that it might "spook" unwary visitors, canine or otherwise, I feel it says a great deal about your character.

But then this is Rugg and Marie.

Was glad to see that Rugg was quite perky despite his injury and was able, in a very limited way, to potter about the house.

After lunch I tried to do the washing up, but Marie is a dear little woman, very much in control and it became clear that I was her guest, and therefore I should not do anything about the house. Normally I would accept this, but I knew that Rugg's injury had placed a great strain upon her since now she was nursing him and trying to do all the chores around the house without any help at all. Part of the reason for my visit was to assist in some way, but it turned out that there really wasn't much I could do, in fact I felt a little embarrassed and annoyed because Marie was bustling about trying to look after me as well as Rugg! I had to be quite sharp with her and say she was making me feel awkward because I'd come to help and now felt like a burden. She did back off a bit and try to include me in doing things, but I still wonder if my visit did her any good.

I think it might have helped Rugg, he seemed in very good spirits and Marie said it was the best he'd looked for a long time. It could, of course, be that the medication is at last kicking in, but whatever the reason, it was good to see.

After my little finger wagging at Marie, on Sunday she did think of a few little jobs for me to do, jobs which she evidently felt she could leave to me and which I could not mess up, like hanging out washing and watering the garden, ostensibly to save her back. Then she had a bright idea:

"I know what you can do!" she said brightly. "We've got that new wheelchair which we haven't been able to try out yet, so perhaps you could get it out of the boot of the car to see how easy it is to manage, and then take your Dad for a little jaunt out as he's been stuck in the house for the past few of weeks."

Fine, I agreed. So we hauled this thing out, wheeled it to the top of the drive, strapped Rugg in, and Marie, Small and Arfer waved us goodbye as I set off down Rectory Drive. Now it is common knowledge that north Wales is noted for its mountains. Indeed, there isn't much of Wales which is what you might call flat, and the area around Rugg's house in Bagillt is no exception.

It was as we encountered the first slope away from Rugg's house, and I found myself leaning backwards, feet just not skidding from the weight of a chairbound Rugg, that I realised that downhill, in its own way, can be just as difficult as uphill. Still, we got to the end of Rectory Drive without mishap, and there we paused. I asked whether I should turn left or right. Rugg hummed and haaed and then decided that left wasn't a very pretty route, but there were some nice views if we went right.

It's funny how we delude ourselves. Up until this moment I believed that I was blessed with common sense, and yet as Rugg made his decision, and my own brain gave me a nudge and said "We've taken a walk along the road to the left before, and we know that, yes, it may be boring, but it's reasonably flat", another part of my brain said: "Ah, poor Rugg, out for the first time in ages, let's look at the views", without thinking of the consequences.

So we turned right, proceeded downhill even more, turned left, and now my eyes were bulging and my arm muscles were twitching with the effort of not letting Rugg hurtle Bagilltwards down an even steeper hill. Just when I thought I was going to have to give in, and was rationalising that perhaps hospital would be the best place for the old fellow anyway, Rugg indicated with his stick that we should go down a little alleyway to the right. We negotiated a couple of motorcycle foilers (you know, two metal barriers that you have to wiggle through) without much injury to leg or chair, and had quite a nice stroll along a very gentle downward slope until we got to a point where we could admire a field full of cows and get a glimpse of the Dee. Much fortified I asked (with the merest tremor in my voice) if we had to go back the way we came, or whether there was another way home. Rugg said, no, if we went just a little further we would come to a pretty little lane that would loop to the right and so back up to Rectory Drive.

It was as we turned the corner and I saw the "pretty little lane" that my nerve almost gave. It rose before me, a one in six at a modest estimate, narrow and winding until after about a couple of hundred yards it turned a corner and out of sight.

We stopped and looked at it.

"Ah," said my father after the silence had lengthened to awkward proportions, "it looks a bit steep, doesn't it?"

My mouth worked. I wondered what the current penalty for patricide was. I wondered - if I did it right - if anyone would actually know it was patricide and not just an unfortunate accident. I wondered how I would console Marie. I wondered (suddenly) if Marie was at home with fingers crossed hoping for just such an "accident". Then

I remembered (with just a touch of irritation) that I was a Christian and that such thoughts did not become me.

"Well," I said, mentally girding my loins and wondering just how painful a hernia was, "we'll have to nibble at it. I'll get you to the first driveway, then have a rest, then make it to the next one and so on until we're at the top."

And with a deep breath, we were off.

I'm not sure how much Rugg weighs. Maybe one ton, maybe two. Either way I was deeply regretting the cake and apple crumble I'd brought with me and which he had enjoyed. I pushed, staring at the ground, watching it inch away with painful slowness beneath my feet. As we went Rugg kindly pointed out the wild flowers growing out of the verge, and noted the song of (he rather thought) a thrush.

I wished I had a shotgun. And not necessarily for the cheery thrush.

We made it to the first driveway and pulled in. I stood with my hands on my knees, gasping for breath, coughing fit to burst while Dad took in the scenery. Once my heartbeat had subsided to a level where I could actually hear again, we set off, and I'll swear that darned hill got a bit steeper. We just made it to the next drive and were now about two thirds of the way up. There was a little wall at this drive and I slumped onto it, hoping that my heart would not actually manage to break its way out of my chest, and waiting for the black swirling spots to go away from before my eyes.

It was at this point our Good Samaritan came along. Or rather, the Good Liverpudlian. A man was walking down the hill and he caught sight of us. Luckily the lane was too narrow for him to pass by on the other side without vaulting a hedge, so he glanced at us, took in my pathetic appearance, slowed down and asked if we needed any help. My pride had long gone, along with my strength and my dignity (I was sitting, legs spread apart, head down, gasping). I would have leapt up and kissed him if I didn't think that such an action by a red-faced, wild-eyed, manically coughing and sweating middle-aged woman would have sent him screaming away from us. I attempted a smile instead, and although he did blench and take an involuntary step backwards at what must have been something very akin to a death's-head grimace, he manfully stood his ground.

"Oh please," I said, trying not to sound too pathetic. "If you could just push my Dad up this last bit to the bend in the road, that would be wonderful."

So, with sickening ease, the good chap took charge of the wheelchair and marched up the last bit of the hill and round the corner to flatter ground, where I took over. Rugg and I finally debouched onto Bryn Tierion Road, cruised down a little, and then up Rectory Drive back home.

When we saw Marie I announced in no uncertain terms: "Marie, NO, you cannot push Dad about in that thing. Maybe if you drive somewhere flat, then take it out and go for a stroll, along a promenade or something to get the sea breezes, maybe. But round here. NO."

So I suppose that in the end it counted as a useful visit.

I made the mistake of telling Ann about my visit.

"Wot Ho to the Old Floral Welly" (*It seems that Ann is really taken with that catalogue she read recently*)

"So, the bottom line is, I gather, that the new antibiotics are starting to have some effect, huh? I think that was mentioned somewhere in the dialogue. Maybe.

There was me worried sick about my poor old Pa. Waiting with baited breath to see if I should rush to his side with a cooling sponge and restorative nip of brandy, and all I get is tales of my sister abandoning Marie to look after her Mutt and selfishly indulging herself with meanderings around the countryside admiring the view and importuning strangers to take over the small task of trundling a shrunken and wizened old man a couple of yards along a path so she can sprawl out on a wall and relax.

Me, me, me – that's all I get nowadays!

So, you're back in the oxygen tent, are you? I must admit, when you started to say that you were going to take the Rugg out for a local airing my mind (seeing as I think in pictures, you understand) immediately did a sweep of the known area of the Ruggery and thought: Hilly. Just one word: Hilly. So there were no surprises when the story unfolded.

But I did note one thing that you missed. You bade goodbye to Arfer. Now Arfer (so rumour has it) is a dog. And there is a certain breed of dog called a Husky. And huskies (you can see where I'm going with this) are used for pulling sledges. QED Arfer could be used for pulling Ruggs. With you up on the back axle, whip flying, shouting 'Mush! Mush!' I think you could get up quite a speed as Arfer throws his considerable weight against the burden of the Enthroned Rugg, and it would certainly be a good way of seeing the countryside.

Anyway, I'm glad that the Aged P enjoyed himself. No doubt he is looking forward to your next visit and is plotting a route around Snowdonia, knowing how much you like spectacular views and nice quite lanes.

Maybe I could suggest a few ......

I'm sure that your visit did Marie a world of good. Laughter is extremely therapeutic, and no doubt she was splitting her sides as she watched you disappear round the curve in the road, knowing what was to come.

Some of it has to be, of course, Your Own Fault (shades of our dear mother coming in here, you notice). What was that about cake and apple crumble? You stoked Rugg up with cake and apple crumble and then wondered why he weighed a couple of tons? You should have done a sneaky and e-mailed Marie that the best cure for cuts was starvation rations of lettuce and radishes for a couple of weeks, and then you would be up with a pack of dogs and a skateboard.

Love twall
Mowl"

It's so refreshing to know that I can always count on sympathy from my nearest and dearest. What would I do without them? As the Great Uncle always says:

"It doesn't matter if life hands you lemons, just so long as they're soaked in a goodly measure of gin and tonic."

And my family is certainly full of lemons. Hand me that gin bottle ......